This is Taking Chances

Wild Child Reckless Book Three

Juliet McKinley

Suddenly Juliet

For the ones still trying. Still staying. Still here. You are worthy. You are loved.

Even on the days it doesn't feel like it.

Prologue

Grayson

I'm five when I decide to hide in the trunk of Dad's car. It's the best hiding spot — cool and dark, just big enough for me to curl up and not get found. The air smells like oil and dust. I tug the lid closed and smile into the quiet.

My sisters' voices float through the yard, counting off but they feel far away. It's perfect here.

Until it isn't.

Dad's voice cuts through the stillness. It's loud and angry, not the usual kind. This is sharper, like broken glass.

"You fucking idiot!"

A door slams... hard. It's like I can hear the house shaking.

I freeze, my heart hammering. If he finds me in the car, I'll be in more trouble than ever. His boots scrape gravel. The car door yanks open. The engine growls to life. I want to scream. To tell him I'm here. But I stay hidden.

Then we're moving.

Fast. Faster than usual. Panic curls in my chest. I push the seat. Crawl forward. Light floods in—too bright.

Dad turns. His eyes land on mine, going wide.

And then...

Crash.

When I wake up, everything is still. Too still. The kind that feels wrong. I don't hear beeping. No machines. No voices. Nothing. Just thick, heavy silence pressing down like a blanket I can't push off. My head pounds and chest burns. My throat aches, but no sound comes when I try to speak.

And then — Mom.

Her face swims into view. Puffy eyes. Her hands are flying — fast, desperate gestures I don't understand.

A nurse walks in and I try to ask what's wrong, but I can't hear her voice. I can't hear anything. Panic crashes through me. I cry. I cry so hard my lungs ache and my vision goes blurry. Doctors come, touching me with cold hands, mouths moving silently.

But all I want is Mom. Thankfully she stays.

Now I'm eight.

I sit in class, staring at the board. I see the chalk move but don't hear the scratch. The room buzzes, but only in feeling — footsteps through the floor, the faint vibration of laughter I can't join.

Mom sits in the back of the room, signing everything as best she can. She's not supposed to be here anymore. But she won't leave until I can keep up on my own.

I used to hate that. Now, I depend on it. Her hands are my anchor. The world is silent, but it's not empty anymore. Her language became mine. And somehow, over time, the silence stopped feeling like a prison.

It became a part of me. By nine, sound is something I used to know. An idea. A ghost I stopped chasing.

There is only silence. And her hands moving in the quiet.

Chapter 1

Grayson

Cora is waiting when we walk into the studio, but it's not just her. A girl stands at her side, shifting from foot to foot, eyes darting like she's trying to memorize every detail. I catch Jensen's glance, and he lifts an eyebrow, already questioning. Delilah just looks curious. Mia doesn't even look up from her phone.

"Guys, this is Madison," Cora says. "She's your PA. Would've been here sooner, but she was finishing some certifications. She's been with Revelation Records for years and will be your point of contact on tour."

The girl clears her throat. ***"Hello, everyone. Like Cora said, I'm Madison, but you can call me Maddie."***

As she speaks, she signs. My gaze snaps to her hands. Delilah gives me the slightest nod, like she knew this was coming. We were told she studied sign language. What catches me isn't that she can sign; it's how she does it. It's smooth, natural, like it's her first language. There is no hesitation, no fumbling.

She's fluent.

Her brown hair curls down around her shoulders, and her glasses slip slightly down her nose. She's nervous but not fragile. Her eyes track the room like she's cataloging it. She's not trying to impress us; she's trying to understand us. Delilah's already talking, her excitement building, but Maddie's attention shifts back to me.

I lift my hands. ***"I'm Grayson. Nice to meet you."***

Her lips tip into a smile. Her reply is smooth and unhesitant. ***"Nice to meet you too."***

Delilah's still gesturing wildly beside Jensen. Maddie follows my gaze, then looks back at me.

"They've been like this forever," I sign, smirking.

Her grin widens. ***"I figured. Have you all played together for a long time?"***

I nod. ***"Jensen, Delilah, and I started Wild Child Reckless a few years ago. It just took off. We've been stuck together ever since."***

She raises her brows. ***"That's impressive. So it hasn't always been the four of you?"***

I shake my head, glancing toward Mia, who is still absorbed in her phone. ***"Mia joined us when we got to L.A. We needed a pianist. Delilah found her singing at a speakeasy nearby. Best decision we made."***

Maddie's eyes flick toward Mia, then back. ***"She seems interesting."***

I huff a laugh. ***"She is. And one of the best musicians I've ever met. She put me in my place, night one. Funny story."***

"I can't wait to hear it."

I study her more closely. There's no strain in the way she signs. No pause between thought and movement. She also observant and quick.

"Do you know much about us?" I sign.

She shrugs, lips twitching. ***"I did some research."***

I arch a brow. ***"Like what?"***

She hesitates, then signs, ***"Your first EP was recorded with Delilah's fourteenth birthday present from her brother. Delilah writes most of the lyrics, but you and Jensen polish them. And your setlists always start the same because Jensen says it 'sets the tone.'"***

My brows rise. ***"You weren't kidding."***

She shrugs again, but there's something pleasing in her eyes. ***"I like to be prepared. If I'm going to work with you, I should know more than the basics."***

I nod slowly, tension bleeding from my shoulders for the first time since we walked in.

This may not be so bad after all.

The house is quiet when I settle onto the couch later in the evening. My phone is in my hand, waiting for the call to connect. A moment later, Mom's face fills the screen. I prop it against a stack of books on the coffee table.

Her features soften instantly. ***"Grayson,"*** she signs. ***"It's late."***

"It's not that late." I stretch out on the cushions. ***"Just got back."***

She gives me a look. ***"You look tired."***

"You always say that."

Her smile fades. Her hands slow. ***"You're going on tour soon."***

"With Gio Santoro," I sign.

She doesn't hide the frown. ***"It's a big step. Bigger venues. More pressure."***

"I can handle it."

"I know." Her hands stall. ***"But I also know the industry. And I know how hard it is for you to communicate sometimes."***

"I've got the band," I reply. ***"And we have a new PA. She signs."***

That gets a pause.

"Really?"

"Fluent," I add. *"She's good."*

Mom watches me for a beat, then nods. *"I just want you to be okay."*

"I will be."

We talk for a few more minutes before I promise to check in again. I end the call and head to the kitchen. The house is dim. I don't expect anyone else to be up.

But Maddie's at the counter, dunking a tea bag into a mug.

She glances up, surprised, then offers a small smile. *"Couldn't sleep?"*

"Something like that." I grab water and lean against the counter. *"You?"*

"Tea helps." She lifts the mug. *"Plus, I like the quiet."*

I nod. *"So you're really coming on tour."*

She smirks. *"That is the job."*

"Ever been on tour before?"

"Not like this." She sips the tea. *"I've worked with artists, but nothing this big."*

"You nervous?"

She thinks, then shakes her head. *"Excited. And ready to work. You?"*

I sigh. *"We've toured, but this is different. Gio is huge, and we're just the openers."*

"Wild Child Reckless isn't small," she says simply. *"A lot of people are showing up for you."*

It's matter-of-fact, not flattery. And it almost makes me smile.

"Your mom's worried about the tour," **she adds.**

I blink. *"Yeah."*

"Because of communication?"

"That. And the rest. Crowds. Hours. The road."

"But you've done this before," she signs. *"And you've got people watching out for you."*

"Including you?"

She arches a brow. *"That is the job."*

I shake my head, smiling despite myself. She's calm. Confident. And not trying too hard.

She rinses her mug and sets it aside. *"We should get some sleep. Big day tomorrow."*

"Yeah." I straighten.

"Goodnight, Grayson."

"Goodnight, Maddie."

She disappears down the hall, and I stand there for a beat longer, holding my breath without meaning to.

Chapter 2
Maddie

After that incredible set, I made sure there's something here for everyone—snacks, drinks, whatever they need. The energy in the room is still electric, humming under everyone's skin. Grayson goes high, Jensen slaps his hands, and then Grayson returns the favor.

"That was amazing!" Grayson signs, face flushed, hands flying. The crowd was loud. The set was tight. They crushed it.

Jensen grabs a water, sweat still dripping down his neck. "Quick shower," he mutters, disappearing into the side room.

I double-check my clipboard. Everything's in place. Still, I keep moving, tidying up here and there. It's easier than standing still.

When Jensen returns, fresh and changed, I hear the sound that makes my stomach turn—giggling. It's high-pitched and too loud.

Grayson is sprawled across a couch, surrounded by three girls in microscopic dresses, red solo cups clutched in manicured hands. They're giggling as he shows them signs, his fingers moving slower than usual, a smirk curling his mouth.

On the table: Jack, Johnny, and José. Perfect.

My grip tightens on the clipboard. It's not jealousy—I barely know him. But something about how he soaks in the attention, how quickly he lets chaos through the door... it grates. He's the drummer, sure, not the spokesperson. But still. We're not even three shows into this leg of the tour, and he's already playing rockstar roulette with girls who couldn't spell Reckless, let alone name a song.

Jensen appears beside me. "Hey, Mads."

I flinch. "Oh. Hey." I pass him his phone. "Grabbed it on the way back."

He nods. Then, he jerks his chin toward the couch. "What's with Barbie, Bimbie, and company?"

I roll my eyes. "They were outside with the booze. I was going to call security, but Grayson waved them in."

Another shriek. My patience thins.

"I'm going to check on Delilah," I mutter. "Let me know when I can take the trash out."

I stalk toward the stage entrance, irritation rising like static. He can do whatever he wants. It's not my problem. Still, I'm boiling. Near the back entrance, I spot Mia. She's off to the side, gripping a folded paper in both hands. Her posture is tight.

"Mia? Everything okay?"

She startles. "Yeah. Nothing."

I tilt my head. "That doesn't look like nothing."

She studies me. Her voice is quieter this time. "Why do you look pissed off?"

I pause. She's not just asking—she's offering. A soft kind of mirror, hoping I'll give something back. But I deflect. Like I always do.

I blink. "I don't."

She doesn't believe me, but she lets it drop. Delilah's coming off the stage, radiant from the performance. She locks eyes with Gio, slipping easily into his orbit as they head toward the green room.

Seconds later, Delilah's scream cuts through the hallway.

That can't be good. I rush back just in time to see three girls bolt past me, yanking their tops into place. Inside the room, Grayson's still on the couch, looking smug. Delilah is livid, her hands flying in a flurry of messy signs. I try to keep up, but she's too fast, too angry.

Grayson chuckles.

Wrong move.

Delilah grabs a pillow and swings.

"Delilah! You're signing it wrong!" I dart forward, trying to intervene.

Too late.

She releases the pillow mid-swing, and I stumble—straight into Grayson's lap. My face ignites. I scramble up, glasses askew.

Delilah blinks. *"What?"*

"You signed it wrong." I adjust my glasses, clearing my throat. *"You said, 'Don't be a donkey; stop dancing, girls.' You meant, 'Don't be dumb, stop chasing girls.' That's why he laughed. Though..."* I mumble, *"he is a bit of an ass."*

Jensen cackles.

Delilah groans. *"Fine. Whatever. But I better not see more of that in my rec room."*

Grayson lifts both hands, exaggerating his innocence, before downing his drink. My phone buzzes. It's one hour until call time.

"Sixty minutes," I announce. *"Figure your shit out."*

I board the bus with tension still tight in my shoulders. Delilah's riding with Gio tonight, so it's just Mia, Jensen, Grayson, and me.

Mia's already curled in her bunk, clutching that same paper. She doesn't look up.

Fine.

Still, I glance back once. She's staring at that note like it might bite. I think about going to her again. But I don't. I collapse onto the couch and pull up Eureka. Science, humor, chaos. Comfort TV. The kind of show you can half-watch and still feel like you're in on the joke. It's my go-to. Predictable. Safe. The opposite of what the last few hours have been. I sink into it, letting the familiar voices wash over me.

Movement in the corner of my eye pulls me back to the moment.

Grayson, hair damp, hoodie hanging loose, drops into the seat beside me.

"You're up late," he signs.

"So are you."

He stretches out. *"What are we watching?"*

"Eureka."

"Cool."

I hesitate. Then: *"Grayson... about earlier."*

His face tightens. I keep going.

"I know it's easy to get swept up. But that stuff? The drinking, the groupies—it can wreck people. You're talented. Don't waste it."

He signs: ***"I don't need a lecture, Mads."***

"Not a lecture. Just... worry. Whether you want it or not."

He sighs. ***"I'm *fine.*"***

Maybe. But he's not convincing. I let it go. No point pushing. I focus on the show. But I still catch myself glancing at him, trying to figure out where the cracks are. He's a walking contradiction—chaos and calm, bravado and stillness. He makes it hard to know which version is real, which unsettles me more than I want to admit.

Then he disappears into the kitchenette. I frown, thinking he's done. He returns with a mug and sets it in front of me.

Chamomile.

I blink. He didn't ask. Didn't check. Just knew.

"You?"

He shrugs and flops back onto the couch.

I reach into the stash of snacks tucked behind the couch cushion and toss his favorites onto the table.

His smirk grows. ***"Thanks."***

I roll my eyes. ***"Yeah, yeah."***

He tosses an M&M in the air, catches it in his mouth, then nudges my leg. It's casual, familiar. It's too familiar for someone who was drinking tequila with strangers an hour ago. It's too comfortable for someone who shouldn't matter.

But he does. Somehow. And that might be the most dangerous part of all.

"Play the next episode."

I shake my head, smiling, and hit play. Outside, the bus hums
against the quiet night. Inside, the screen flickers, casting a soft
light over us. And for the first time all day, I feel like I can breathe
again.

Chapter 3
Grayson

The crowd's energy slams into me like a wave—lights flashing, vibrations running up my arms from the kick drum, the heat sharp under my skin. We crash into the final note, and I grin, sweat dripping from my temple.

Delilah spins her guitar around her back, then turns and holds up three fingers.

Encore.

Off to the side, Maddie signs the title.

"Shooting Tequila."

Of course.

I huff a breath through my nose and get ready.

The crowd loves this one, but Delilah feels it differently. She wrote it about Alexander, her brother's best friend, the guy who pretends not to look at her like she's air after drowning. She says she's moved on. Mia says she's trying.

But songs don't lie.

I shift in my seat, letting the weight of the sticks anchor me. The lights flash, warm against my skin, and the crowd's roar is a living thing I feel rather than hear. When the first downbeat hits, it's not just the song—it's gravity. My chest vibrates from the sub, every pulse in time with the thrum in my veins. This is the only place where everything makes sense.

I tap the sticks together, start the count-in, and the song crashes in like instinct. Three hours on stage, and I could still play another three. Now that we're headlining, every set is a full sprint. And I love it.

Later, we pile into the rec room backstage, buzzing with sweat and adrenaline. Jensen's halfway into a victory beer, retelling part of the set with loud gestures. Delilah flops into a beanbag, still glowing. Someone's got a playlist blasting from a Bluetooth speaker that can barely handle the bass.

I towel off and scan the room.

Maddie's on the edge of the couch, legs tucked, hands tight around a water bottle. Her clipboard's not in sight, which is rare. She looks like she's waiting for something. She's watching

Jensen laugh and Delilah shout-sing over the speaker. Her fingers tap the water bottle in a steady rhythm like she's holding herself still on purpose. Not bored. Just... bracing.

I head over and drop beside her—close, but not too close.

"You okay?"

"Yeah," she signs. *"Just tired. You were incredible tonight."*

Her signs are clean but slower than usual. Like she's forcing her brain to keep up with her hands. I wonder if she ever lets herself stop being responsible. Or if that clipboard is just a shield she never puts down.

"Thanks."

She smiles, but it's tight. Her eyes dart toward the others.

"What's your plan tonight?" she asks aloud.

"Not sure yet. You?"

"Order something. Trash TV. Try to sleep before 2."

"That sounds better than the bar."

Her brows rise. *"Seriously? You're skipping a band night for pad thai and bad reality shows?"*

"If there's mango sticky rice."

She laughs—real, startled. Like it caught her off guard.

Back at the hotel, the floor's littered with takeout containers. The TV throws flickering light across the bedspread. Maddie's cross-legged, clipboard forgotten, and she looks settled for the first time in days.

There's something weirdly peaceful about the hotel room. After all that sound and movement, the hush feels earned. I've ended nights like this before—parties, hookups, bad choices that felt good at the moment. This? This is something else. Like I'm resting without needing to recover.

Halfway through the second episode, I nudge her arm.

"Can I see your clipboard?"

She blinks. *"What?"*

"Your clipboard," I repeat, deadpan. *"I just... I need to know if it's permanently attached."*

She laughs and hands it over. *"Be careful. It holds the universe together."*

I flip it open and make a face. *"So many tabs. I think it bit me."*

She rolls her eyes, but her shoulders drop a little. *"Give it back."*

"Eventually."

We fall into quiet again, and then she turns from the TV.

"Can I ask you something personal?"

I nod.

"Why drums?"

"I was supposed to be a football prodigy," I sign.

Her eyebrows lift.

"Quarterback. Strong arm. College interest by fifteen. But I was deaf, and that didn't fit. My dad stopped looking me in the eye after junior year."

She's silent, watching.

"Mom's deaf too. She got it. Always did. But Dad... he checked out." I shift. *"I found drums in middle school. No words. Just rhythm. They made sense."*

"You don't talk about it much," she says.

"Most people don't ask."

She holds my gaze. *"Well. I'm not most people."*

And somehow, I believe her.

"What about you? What did you want to be before you became the clipboard queen?"

She snorts and signs it back. *"Clipboard queen."* Then she shifts.

"My family has a ranch in Northern California. I was supposed to stay and take it over with my brothers, but

I wanted something else, so I applied to college without telling anyone."

Her signs are so clean and expressive, like language that lives in her whole body.

"I took every ASL class I could, minored in event logistics, and thought I'd end up in a conference center."

"Instead, you got us," I sign.

"A wild ride," she replies.

"You ever miss the ranch?"

"Sometimes," she signs. *"The quiet mornings. The stars. But not the part where I had to stay small."*

I nod. *"Yeah. I get that."*

We sit there, hands still, but it's comfortable. She stretches out, her toes brushing mine under the blanket. She doesn't move. Neither do I.

"Did you ever think you'd end up here?" she asks.

I shake my head. *"We were killing it at home. But this? Tour buses? Cities screaming our lyrics? Never imagined."*

She watches me. Present. Open.

"Still, I wonder how I'm still here some nights. How I got lucky enough to be standing after everything."

"You earned it," she signs. *"You didn't wait for permission. You built it."*

It lands. Heavy. Real.

"Most people just see the noise. The stage. That I'm deaf and play drums."

"That's not what I see." Her hands are steady. *"You're more than that."*

I don't know what to say. She shifts again, her toes nudging mine—on purpose this time.

"I used to think connection came from shared experience," she adds. *"But I feel more seen in silence with you than I ever did in the noise."*

My chest tightens. Not in a bad way. I reach for her hand, brushing my fingers against hers.

"I see you too."

She links our fingers and moves our hands beneath the blanket.

No declarations. No kiss. Just quiet. And this, this moment, this stillness, is going to be the thing I remember long after the tour ends. And for once, it's enough.

Chapter 4
Maddie

The band's been headlining for six months, and already, the cities are starting to blur. Backstage hallways all smell vaguely the same: sweat, stale popcorn, and that sharp tang of electrical wires overheating. I keep a running list on my phone—city, venue, anything distinct to keep them straight. But most nights, remembering where we are still takes me a minute.

Tonight, it's a mid-sized amphitheater packed wall to wall. Six thousand seats, maybe more. The kind of crowd that buzzes like static before the lights even dim.

And when they do? Chaos.

Concession lines spill into reception. People crowd the security barrier, singing every lyric like it belongs to them. It's loud, electric, and alive. I'm offstage, standing where the shadows meet the curtain's edge, clipboard in hand, watching for anything that might throw the set off course. Lighting glitch.

Feedback hum. A cue Jensen forgets to hit again. But mostly, I'm watching Grayson.

He's slick with sweat, his curls damp and sticking to his forehead, and his grin is stretched wide across his face. He plays like he was born with drumsticks in his hands, like rhythm lives in his bones. He's in perfect sync with the rest of the band, never missing a beat, even when the tempo shifts or the crowd roars loud enough to rattle the stage.

No one watching him would guess he's deaf. It took him years of relentless practice, muscle memory, vibration, and instinct to master what he makes look effortless. But I know. I've seen the work. The frustration. The way he'll run a fill again and again until he feels it click into place.

So I may focus more on him than the others.

Delilah and Jensen are at the front of the stage, feeding off each other's energy, performing like they were born to be in the spotlight. They're damn good at it too. The crowd screams louder when they move together—Delilah winking mid-verse, Jensen hitting a perfectly timed harmony. The fans lose their minds.

But it's Grayson I watch.

Always Grayson.

Because I know that if something changes—a sudden light cue, a missed transition, a call from the tech crew, I have to tell him. He's counting on me to make sure he doesn't get blindsided. And maybe he doesn't say it, but I know he trusts me to catch it. To catch him. So I keep watching. And I keep my hands ready.

The show ends in a flood of cheers and buzzing adrenaline. When I make it to the rec room, the party is already well underway.

Grayson's leaning against the arm of a couch, a glass of whiskey in hand, groupies draped on either side of him like they belong there. One of them is giggling at something he didn't say. He looks up and sees me but doesn't move. He just grins—loose and bright, like the weight of the stage is still thrumming in his veins.

I ignore the twist in my chest.

He's allowed to do whatever he wants. I'm not here to monitor his personal life. I'm here to keep the band functioning, the schedule tight, the chaos contained. Delilah and Jensen are already deep into their second drinks, laughing too loud. The speakers are blasting some remix Jensen swears he loves even though I know he added it to the playlist ten minutes ago. The energy is veering toward recklessness.

I glance at the time and start mentally prepping to shut it all down before someone breaks something we'll have to pay for.

And then the door swings open. Gio steps inside like a storm wrapped in swagger. The room reacts like he walked on stage instead of through a backstage hallway—cheers, shrieks, someone even claps. Delilah all but throws herself across the room into his arms.

He barely glances at the rest of us before signaling to his security, who move with quick, efficient purpose.

"Clear it out," Gio says, smiling like he's not issuing a command.

The room empties in seconds. Delilah clings to him, laughing, and before I can look away, she's climbing him like a tree, mouth on his neck as he chuckles and lifts her without effort. They disappear down the hallway, and the rest of us trail behind. Jensen throws an arm around a tech and heads for the parking lot.

I pause, scanning for Grayson.

He's still near the couch, his drink abandoned, watching the door like he hasn't decided what comes next. I walk up to him, hesitant despite telling myself his answer doesn't matter. ***"Hey,***

are you coming over? I was going to order food. Finish that show we started." For a second, I think he might say yes.

But then he shakes his head, the grin returning. ***"Going out with Jensen. Hitting the bar."***

"Right," I sign, nodding. ***"Of course."***

I smile. Professional. Casual. Like it doesn't sting. Because it shouldn't. Because it's none of my business. Grayson claps me gently on the shoulder, already turning away. And I'm left with a half-typed food order, a show paused in a hotel room, and the echo of something I never had before.

It's two in the morning when there's a knock at my door. It's not quiet either—more like the kind someone makes when trying to stay upright. I drag myself out of bed, blinking through the blur of sleep as I pad across the carpet in a cami and shorts set. The second I crack the door open, I catch sight of Grayson leaning against the frame, swaying slightly, a sheepish grin plastered across his face.

He's drunk. Clearly. Sloppily. His curls are a mess, his eyes glassy, and he's got hickeys blooming on the side of his neck like bruised fruit. He squints at me, then signs, *"You look great. But where are the Rainbow Brite pajamas?"*

I blink. *"What the hell do you want, Grayson?"*

He pats his pockets in a dramatic, slow-motion pantomime and then signs, *"I lost my key. Or maybe Jensen has it. Or a raccoon. I don't know."*

I sigh. *"I don't have your key. Go to the front desk, show your ID, and they'll give you a new one."*

He scrunches his face like I've suggested a ten-mile hike in the snow. *"Too far. Can I stay here instead?"*

I cross my arms, narrowing my eyes. *"Seriously?"*

He gives me the most pathetic, hopeful expression I've ever seen. *"I promise I won't throw up on your shoes. Or hit on you. Much."*

I sigh, already caving, because it's Grayson, and I'm tired, and I know how this ends anyway. *"Fine,"* I sign, stepping aside. *"But you're drinking water and taking aspirin first."*

"Bossy," he responds with a lazy grin as he stumbles past me.

"You're welcome," I add, grabbing a bottle of water and the mini travel bottle of painkillers from my kit.

He downs both without protest and then crawls into the far side of the bed like it's the most natural thing in the world. I turn off the lamp, settle beside him—barely on my side—and close my eyes.

I don't say anything. And neither does he.

Chapter 5

Grayson

Six months later

The bass pulses through the floor, a steady vibration that climbs up my legs as I lean against the bar, a bottle of whiskey dangling from my fingers. The afterparty is in full swing, flashes of movement, bodies packed tight, mouths open in conversation I can't hear. Lights strobe across the room, throwing everything into sharp, fleeting clarity before plunging it back into shadow.

Same scene, different city. Booze, girls, laughter, just another night on the road like every night for the last year. I should be soaking it in. This is what I wanted, right? The rush of touring, the endless parties, the attention. The kind of life that used to feel unobtainable. Now it's mine.

So why does it feel so fucking empty? Maddie's words linger. ***"Too much too fast, and it can wreck people."***

She said it that night six months ago when I knocked on her door at two in the morning, too drunk to find my key, too tired to keep pretending I had everything under control. I crashed in her bed and didn't touch her. She didn't say a word the next morning. Just handed me a coffee and told me to shower before call time.

We never talked about it. We never talk about a lot of things.

Some blonde slides up next to me, her fingers trailing over my arm. Her lips move, but she's not facing me enough for me to catch it, and I don't bother asking her to repeat herself. Instead, she laughs, Fclearly at whatever she said and I couldn't hear, but I nod anyway, letting her think I'm in on the joke.

I take a long drink, letting the burn chase away the thoughts circling in my head. But it doesn't work. My gaze drifts like it always does. And there she is.

Maddie.

Tucked in the corner, clipboard in her lap, watching. Not in an obvious way. She's too good for that. She stays on the edges, pretending she's focused on work, the schedule, and anything but me. But I know better. She's watching me.

And I hate how much I notice.

Because the worst part? She doesn't even look disappointed anymore. Just resigned. Like this is who I am and always will be, and she's already made peace with it.

The bottle in my hand is half-empty when a girl stumbles toward me. Dark hair, blood-red lips, a dress so tight it looks painted on. She smells like vanilla and cheap vodka, and when she smiles, it's slow and deliberate, like she knows exactly what she's doing. She says something, but her words are messy, and her mouth is lazy and unfocused from too many drinks. I have to concentrate, piecing it together as she sways.

"Grayson... you look like you need some fun."

I smirk. Fun. That's the whole point of these parties, isn't it? A distraction. A way to make the endless nights on the road blur together into something that doesn't feel so fucking lonely. She plucks the bottle from my fingers, taking a slow sip before tilting her head back and exposing her throat. Then she speaks again, lips shaping words I have to track carefully.

"Do a shot... off me?"

Someone nearby whoops. I don't hear it, but I catch the movement, the way people react, and the surge of excitement rippling through the group. Just like that, I don't care that her words are a mess, that I have to work twice as hard to follow along. I grab a lime, salt, and a shot of tequila. She giggles as I trail salt along the curve of her collarbone, her breath hitching when I press my tongue to her skin. The shot burns going down, and I chase it with the lime, my teeth grazing her wrist as I pull away.

It doesn't help. My chest still feels hollow. The laughter is noise I can't process, her touch is static, and even the sharp and hot tequila doesn't warm anything but my throat. I want to care. I want to want this. But the truth is, I'm trying too hard to feel something. She shivers, fingers tangling in my hair as she says something else—slurred, lazy. I don't catch all of it, but I don't need to.

"Dance with me."

I don't hear the music shift, but I feel the energy change—the way the people around us move, the heavier pulse of bass rattling the walls. She turns, pressing her back against my chest, body rolling against mine, her hands gripping my wrists, guiding them lower.

I don't think. I don't hesitate. Maddie's words don't belong here.

I turn the girl around, catching pieces of her breathless invitation as she tugs me down for a messy kiss. Her lips form the words I already expect.

"Let's go somewhere."

I don't answer; I just take her hand and lead her toward one of the empty rooms. The party fades behind us, swallowed by the pounding of my pulse.

I don't look back.

I don't need to.

I already know Maddie is watching.

The bus hums beneath my feet, steady and familiar as we roll down another highway toward another city. The afterparty is behind me, but the alcohol still lingers, dulling the edges of my thoughts. I should crash. Sleep off the haze. Instead, I head for the tiny bathroom, stripping out of my sweat-damp clothes and stepping under the spray.

The water is hot, nearly scalding, but I let it run over me, washing away the touch of hands I don't care about and the taste of kisses I barely remember. The haze has cleared by the time I step out, towel slung over my shoulders. The door creaks as I push it open, steam curling into the dimly lit lounge. Maddie is already curled up on the couch, her knees tucked to her chest, waiting.

For me.

For us.

Season three of *Eureka*. The last episode was a cliffhanger. We started this routine months ago, binging it between shows, between miles, between moments when neither of us admits we need something steady to hold onto. She glances up when she sees me, the glow from the TV casting soft shadows over her face. But something's off. The usual spark in her eyes isn't there.

Her fingers toy with the edge of the blanket draped over her lap, twisting the fabric between them.

I don't have to ask to know something's wrong. It's in the tightness of her shoulders, the way she doesn't meet my eyes for more than a second.

I ask anyway. ***"What's wrong?"***

She hesitates, then shakes her head. ***"Nothing."***

Liar.

I could push. Call her on it. But if Maddie doesn't want to talk, she won't. And I'm not in the mood to chase answers she isn't ready to give. Instead, I sigh and drop onto the couch beside her. The blanket shifts as I pull it over my legs, my shoulder pressing into hers like it always does. The warmth of her seeps into me, familiar and steady, like how she always has my soda waiting before I even ask or how she remembers which snacks I like before I do.

Neither of us says anything as she hits play.

The episode picks up where the last one left off, with characters moving and lips forming words I follow out of habit. But my focus drifts. Maddie shifts slightly beside me, and before I realize it, her head rests against my shoulder. I glance down, but she doesn't move; her breaths are slow and even.

Asleep.

I should wake her. Should nudge her toward her bunk and pretend this doesn't mean anything.

But I don't.

Instead, I adjust, pulling the blanket higher and letting my arm settle around her shoulders. She shifts slightly in her sleep like she's used to this now. Like my body is a space she's grown comfortable in, even if neither of us has said it out loud. And that's what wrecks me. She trusts me like this when I'm not sure I trust myself. Her body molds against mine, soft and warm, and for the first time tonight, something in my chest unlocks. I let my head fall back against the couch, staring at the screen but not really watching.

What if?

The thought creeps in, uninvited.

What if Maddie wasn't just my friend, my PA, the person who keeps my life from falling apart?

What if I kissed her, just once, just to see?

What if I woke up tomorrow and stopped pretending she wasn't the best part of this whole damn tour?

The episode rolls on, the flickering light from the TV dancing over the walls, but I don't move.

Not yet.

Chapter 6
Maddie

I barely have my coffee in hand before Delilah slides into the seat across from me, eyes alight with mischief.

"So," she drawls, stirring sugar into her latte. "Are we finally going to talk about whatever's going on between you and Grayson?"

I nearly choke. "What?"

She smirks. "Come on, Mads. You two are practically joined at the hip. Movie nights. Shared blankets. The fact that he gets your tea right every time. It's gross and adorable."

I roll my eyes, trying to hide the blush heating my face. "We're just friends."

"Friends who snuggle," she counters. "Friends who make eyes at each other across afterparties. Friends who would rather hang out together on the bus than go out."

My stomach twists. Not because she's wrong, but because I wish she was.

"We're comfortable," I say. "That doesn't mean it's anything."

Delilah leans back, unconvinced. "Sure. Keep telling yourself that. Just don't be surprised when it starts to hurt."

I open my mouth, but she changes the subject before I can argue.

"You coming out with us tonight?"

I shake my head. "Nope. Bookstore run."

She grins. "You are such a nerd."

"Proud of it," I say, smiling back. But her words linger.

Just don't be surprised when it starts to hurt.

The bookstore is quiet and warm, and the smell of paper and old coffee calms me in a way nothing else can. I wander the aisles and peruse the shelves for a while before a voice beside me says, "That's a good one."

I turn to find a tall, well-dressed man smiling at me. Dark hair, soft eyes. Confident. Easy.

We talk. About books. About the city. Nothing and everything. His name is Ethan. He's a doctor. He's charming and effortless, making me forget how long it's been since someone looked at me like that. He gives me his number although I'm not sure I'll use it, and I give him mine. But when I leave the store, I feel lighter.

The hotel hallway is quiet—until I round the corner and nearly run straight into Grayson. He's not alone.

There's a girl on his arm, barely dressed, clinging to him like she's already memorized the way to his bed. She says something in his ear, but he's not even looking at her. He's looking at me.

"He can't hear you, ya know. He's deaf." I don't even try to hide the snark in my tone, and the girl glares at me and stumbles in her too-high heels.

"What's your problem?" she slurs, and I can't help but roll my eyes.

"We're leaving early," I sign annoyed. ***"Don't forget."***
He waves me off with a lazy nod. ***"Yeah, yeah."***
And just like that, she's tugging him away. I force a smile and keep walking.

Later, in my room, the wall between us is too thin. I hear it. The giggles. The creaking mattress. The muffled rhythm of something I don't want to picture but can't help imagining.

My phone buzzes.

Ethan: *I hope your bookstore haul was a success. What did you end up getting?*

I stare at the screen, desperate for distraction.

Me: *A little of everything. Your rec is on top of the pile.*

The reply comes quick.

Ethan: *Can't wait to hear what you think. Maybe over coffee?*

I close my eyes, trying to breathe past the sound of someone else's pleasure through the wall. I want to say yes. I want different. Because this? This pretending I'm fine while the guy I can't stop thinking about is busy with someone else? It's slowly ripping me apart.

Different is exactly what I need.

The following day, the sun is barely up when I ring the alert system on his door. We learned pretty early on most hotels were not equipped with wake-up systems for deaf rockstars, so we bought one to keep with us on tour. It's come in handy several times due to Grayson's nocturnal activities, especially lately. I lay on the button aggressively; we're supposed to be loading up in thirty minutes, and he's still not answering the door.

The door creaks open.

And she's there. The girl from last night. Her hair's a mess, her makeup smudged, and she's barely wrapped in one of the hotel's towels. Her eyes widen slightly, like she expected housekeeping, not me. "Oh," she says, blinking. "Hi?"

My spine stiffens. "Is Grayson awake?"

She glances over her shoulder at me while walking back to the bed to shake him. "Grayson, babe, someone's here for you."

I hear a groan from inside the room. The unmistakable sound of rustling sheets. That's all I need. I turn on my heel and walk away, chest tight, heart pounding. I can feel the heat crawling up my neck, shame and something bitter rising. Of course, that's how this morning goes. A few minutes later, I'm outside by the bus, clipboard in hand, pretending I didn't just see what I saw.

Pretending I'm not unraveling. When Grayson finally shows up, hoodie pulled low and sunglasses hiding his face, he gives me a halfhearted nod.

I don't return it.

He lifts his hands like he might sign something. Might explain. Might apologize. Might lie. But nothing comes out. So I look past him, down at my notes.

"Everyone's already on. We're waiting on you." And that's all I say.

Later, when the bus is rolling and the others are sleeping or distracted—I find him in the small kitchenette, sipping water like it'll undo the night before. I lean against the counter, arms crossed.

"You could've at least had the decency to be on time," I say, as soon as I have his full attention. He glances up, eyes heavy, motioning for me to repeat. I slow down, signing clearly. ***"You could've at least been on time."***

His response is sluggish. He signs back, ***"Hungover. It happens."***

"Right." My jaw tightens. ***"And the girl in your room? That just happens too?"***

Grayson sighs, pulling off his sunglasses and setting them on the counter. He signs slowly, deliberately. ***"Is this about the schedule or something else?"***

I blink, stunned by the brush-off. *"Do you think I'm upset because you missed the call time?"*

He shrugs, one-handed. *"You're the one who brought it up."*

"God, Grayson. You brought a stranger back to your room. I was standing right there, and you didn't even—"

He cuts me off with a sharp sign. *"What do you want me to say, Maddie? That it meant something? It didn't."*

That hits harder than it should. I swallow, then sign, slower this time. *"Yeah. I got that loud and clear."*

I don't wait for him to say anything else. I just walk away. I duck into the back lounge, pretending to organize my notes, pretending I'm not shaking. The sting of his words settles deep—ugly and hollow. I lean against the wall, fists clenched, and force myself to breathe through it.

He didn't owe me anything. I know that. But that doesn't make it hurt less. My phone buzzes beside me on the seat.

Ethan: *Hope your morning's better than mine. Got called in early. I really wanted to see you before you left. Coffee raincheck?*

I stare at the screen, the ache in my chest still fresh, still burning. But for once, I don't want to sit in it.

I want out. I want something else. Something good.

Me: *Definitely. Let me know when you're free. I'd love that. We're headed to Cinci but it could be a video date.*

The bus hums beneath me, the road a steady rhythm that doesn't care what's falling apart inside. It's not a cure. Not even close. But it's something to hold onto. And right now, that's enough.

Chapter 7

Grayson

The bus rumbles under me, the steady vibrations sinking into my bones as I tap a rhythm against my thigh. It's instinct at this point—fingers drumming out patterns, searching for something to anchor me. Usually it works. Usually I can lose myself in the beat and let it drown out whatever's rattling around in my head.

Not tonight.

Maddie sits across from me, curled up in the lounge with her phone in her lap. She hasn't looked up in at least twenty minutes, too caught up in whatever conversation she's having. Every few seconds, her fingers move, a small smile pulling at the corner of her mouth. It's not the polite smile she gives the crew or the exasperated one she throws at Delilah when she's being dramatic. It's softer. The kind of smile she doesn't even realize she's making.

The kind of smile that makes my stomach twist. I roll my drumsticks between my fingers, keeping my expression neutral.

I don't know who she's talking to. I don't know why I care. But I do. I wait for her to glance up, to acknowledge me like she usually does. But she doesn't.

Instead, she chuckles, shaking her head at something on the screen.

I set my sticks down against the table with too much force and then lifting my hands. *"Who are you talking to?"*

Maddie startles, blinking like she forgot I was even here. She hesitates before signing back. *"Just... a friend."*

I arch a brow. *"A friend?"*

Her lips press together like she knows where this is going. *"Yes, Grayson. A friend."*

I tilt my head, watching her. *"You've been talking to them a lot."*

She shrugs, but there's color in her cheeks. *"His name is Ethan. We met at a bookstore a few days ago."*

Ethan. I don't like it. I don't know Ethan, and I don't know anything about him, but I already don't like it.

"What does he do?"

Maddie rolls her eyes like I'm being ridiculous, but she humors me. *"He's a doctor. A pediatrician, actually."*

A doctor. That's new. The guys she usually talks to are roadies or music fans who exist in our world. This is different. I nod slowly, stretching my legs out. *"Okay. Just be careful."*

Maddie frowns, confused. *"Be careful?"*

I hold her gaze. *"You don't know him. He could be lying to you. Maybe he just wants to get close to the band."*

Her expression shifts, soft confusion turning to something colder. She stares at me, lips parting like she's about to say something, but then she laughs, but her eyes are cold shaking her head. It's not amused. It's bitter.

"That's what you think? That the only reason someone would be interested in me is because of Wild Child Reckless?"

I lift my hands to respond but she steamrolls right over me.

"Do you think I can't possibly meet a guy who actually likes me for me? Maybe he likes talking to me. Maybe he thinks I'm funny. Maybe, God forbid, he actually finds me attractive."

I scramble to backtrack. *"Maddie, that's not what I meant...."*

But she shakes her head, standing abruptly. *"No. Just because you don't want me doesn't mean no one else ever will."*

The words hit like a sudden cymbal crash, leaving me reeling.

I watch as she grabs her phone and disappears into the bunk area, the door shutting behind her.

I sit there for a long moment, jaw clenched, fingers twitching for my sticks. I didn't mean to insult Maddie. Didn't mean to make it sound like I don't see her—like I don't want her.

But maybe that's the real problem.

Because I do.

And now I wonder if I ensured she'll never see me the same way.

I sit in the lounge, one leg bouncing, my eyes flicking toward the hallway where the bunks are. *Warehouse 13* is queued up on the TV, waiting for Maddie. We finally finished *Eureka* last week; now this is our new thing. It's routine, comfortable, something to look forward to after long days on the road.

But she's not here.

Frowning, I grab my phone and text her. No answer.

Okay. Something's wrong.

I push up from the couch, making my way toward her bunk. The curtain is drawn tight, with no light peeking through. I hesitate briefly before pulling it open just enough to peek inside.

Maddie is curled up on her side, her back to me, shoulders shaking slightly. Shit.

I climb in without a word, stretching out beside her in the cramped space. She stiffens but doesn't move away. I curl behind her, resting one arm gently around her waist, forehead against the back of her head.

For a moment, we just lie there, breathing in sync.

Then I shift, pulling back enough so she can see me. I prop myself on one elbow, catching her wrist to get her attention.

"Hey,." I sign against her skin, then wait for her to turn.

Slowly, she rolls to face me, her eyes red but steady. *"What's wrong?"* I ask.

"Nothing," she signs.

I raise a brow. *"That's a lie."*

She huffs. *"It's stupid."*

"I'm stupid a lot." I try to soften it with a smile. *"Tell me anyway."*

Her fingers move hesitantly. *"Just because you don't want me doesn't mean someone won't someday. But it still hurts."*

My chest tightens. I reach out, curling my hand around hers before she can pull back.

"Maddie, stop." I hold her gaze, my signs deliberate. *"You're beautiful. You're worth wanting. Anyone would be lucky to have you."*

Her throat bobs. *"You don't have to say that just to make me feel better."*

"I'm saying it because it's true." I hesitate, my fingers brushing hers. *"I hate that I made you feel like you weren't."*

She doesn't answer. But she doesn't let go either. She just lets me stay.

I shift closer, tucking her against my chest, letting my arms wrap around her. She doesn't fight it. Instead, she exhales, shaky and soft, and buries her face against my shoulder.

After a while, I grab her iPad from the little ledge beside her bed and pull up *Warehouse 13*. She blinks at me, confused.

"Are you coming out, or are we watching in here?"

A small smile tugs at her lips. *"Here's fine."*

I press play, the two of us curled up in the tiny bunk, the screen's glow flickering over us. Before long, her breathing evens out, and I follow soon after, both of us tucked away from the rest of the world, safe in this small space together.

I wake to warmth. Soft, steady breaths against my chest, a weight curled into my side. For a second, I don't move or open my eyes—just let myself exist in this quiet, unfamiliar moment. The smell of cotton and ink swirls in the air.

Then reality settles in.

Maddie.

She's tucked against me, her hand resting lightly on my shoulder, her hair fanned over my chest. I stare at her, her features softened in sleep, her lips slightly parted. She's peaceful, untouched by the chaos that usually follows us on the road.

I'm not used to waking up next to someone without a hangover dulling the edges, without the immediate regret or the quiet scramble to disengage before things get awkward. But this?

This feels different.

I lift a hand, careful, hesitant, and brush a stray curl from her face. She shifts slightly, nuzzling into me, and something profound in my chest tightens.

I don't know what this is. I just know I don't want to move.

Chapter 8
Maddie

I lean against one of the road cases, watching as the opening band loads out. I don't know if they picked their own name or if the label cursed them with it, but either way, The Velvet Pickles will have a rough time being taken seriously.

"Do you think they know?" I ask, tilting my head toward Jensen as he coils up a stray cable.

Grayson stands next to me, arms crossed over his chest. He follows my gaze before flicking his eyes back to me. ***"Know what?"***

"That 'The Velvet Pickles' is a terrible name."

Grayson's face stays neutral for half a second before his lips twitch. ***"Maybe they think it's ironic."***

"They have a song called 'Brined for Your Pleasure,' Grayson." That does it. His shoulders shake as he presses a hand over his face to hide his laughter. I grin, pleased with myself, but my amusement fades as my eyes drift back to Jensen. The groupies are still here—because of course they are.

Wild Child Reckless is headlining now, and some things don't change. Girls will always flock to Jensen and Grayson, drawn in by the music, the tattoos, and how they look under stage lights. Jensen leans back against the bar in the green room, a lazy smile on his face as two girls drape themselves over him. He says something that makes them giggle, the picture of easy confidence. But then he turns away for a moment, and I see it.

That moment where his face falls.

It's quick, just a breath. His shoulders sag the usual spark in his eyes flickering out before he reaches for his beer and takes a long pull. It's subtle, but I know Jensen. He's drinking more than usual. And when he thinks no one's looking, he isn't smiling. A nudge against my arm pulls me from my thoughts. I glance over to see Grayson watching me. ***"You see it too?"***

I nod, my stomach twisting. ***"Yeah."***

Grayson taps his fingers against his thigh, his gaze flicking back to Jensen. ***"We should keep an eye on him."***

I exhale, crossing my arms. ***"Yeah. We should."***

Because something is wrong. And I'm not about to ignore it.

The energy in the venue is electric, the kind that hums in your bones and lingers even after the last note fades. Wild Child Reckless is wrapping up their set, the final chords of their encore ringing through the air. From my spot offstage, I watch as Grayson pounds out the last few beats on his drums, sweat dampening the ends of his hair. Jensen and Delilah lean into each other at center stage, guitars slung low, feeding off the crowd's roar one last time.

The crowd is deafening. Chicago always brings it. I shift my weight from foot to foot, my phone buzzing in my back pocket. A text from Ethan:

Ethan: *How's the show? Should I be jealous?*

I bite my lip, smiling as I type back.

Me: *Incredible, as usual. And maybe. Grayson's drum solo was pretty sexy tonight.*

Ethan: *Damn. Be honest, Maddie. Did he outshine me?*

Me: *Idk, you might need to work a little harder.*

Ethan and I have been texting on and off since we met here eight months ago. Life kept getting in the way between his shifts at the hospital and me being constantly on the road. He briefly dated someone. It didn't last. I haven't dated anyone at all. Lately, our conversations have been veering into what-if territory. What if we lived in the same city? What if we actually went on a real date?

Jensen's voice cuts in, slinging an arm around my shoulder as he passes by. "We're hitting up Jake's after this. You in?"

Jake's. Of course. Cheap drinks, good music, and just enough grime to make it feel like home.

"Yeah, I'm in," I say, pulling out my phone.

Me: *We're going to Jake's. Come out.*

Ethan: *Maddie, are you asking me on a date?*

Me: *I'm asking you to have a drink with me. Don't ruin it.*

Ethan: *I'd love to, but I'm working, remember?*

My stomach dips. I should've remembered.

Me: *Right. Forgot you had a real job.*

Ethan: *Ouch. I'll have you know saving tiny humans is essential work.*

Me: *Yeah, yeah. Some excuse.*

Ethan: *Next time, Maddie. Promise.*

I roll my eyes but smile, tucking my phone away and letting the band pull me into the post-show buzz.

The bar is packed. The air is thick with spilled beer, sweat, and the low thrum of bass vibrating through the floor. I stir the ice in

my water with my straw, watching Delilah lean over the jukebox, arguing with someone about the next song. Jensen is nursing his whiskey, gaze distant even with two girls hovering nearby. And Grayson—well, Grayson is pretending not to notice the girl in his lap, clearly determined to get his attention.

I smile, shaking my head as a voice cuts through the noise.

"You look like you could use something stronger than that."

I whip around, my heart stalling.

Ethan.

He slides onto the stool beside me, thigh brushing mine, his warmth bleeding through my jeans. "Got someone to cover my shift," he says, eyes locking onto mine. "Figured I couldn't let you drink alone."

A slow smile spreads across my lips. "Oh, so now you're trying?"

He leans in, the scent of his cologne warm and clean. His voice drops. "Maddie, I've been trying."

The air crackles.

He orders drinks: something dark and burning for him and something smoother for me. The conversation flows easily, playful and threaded with something new. Every brush of his fingers against mine sends heat coiling low in my belly. Every look lingers longer than the last.

And then we dance.

The music is slow and sultry. It wraps around us like smoke. His hands settle on my waist, sure and steady. His body moves with mine like he already knows how. His breath skims my neck, and I shiver.

"You've been holding out on me," I whisper.

His fingers flex, pulling me closer. His lips ghost my temple. "Maybe I just needed the right incentive."

I grip his shirt, unable to stop myself. The air between us hums, charged and bright.

"Come back to my hotel."

His jaw tightens. "Maddie..."

He's not saying no. He's just giving me a chance to.

"Unless you don't want to," I say, voice barely audible.

His eyes darken. "Let's go."

We don't walk so much as pull each other through the city like something inevitable. His hand is at my back, his mouth brushing my ear with promises I can't hear. The elevator is too slow. The tension is a taut string between us.

The moment we're in the room, the air shifts.

He presses me against the door, one hand braced beside my head, the other tracing my jaw. Watching me. Waiting.

I grab his shirt and pull him in.

The kiss is fire, no hesitation, no slow burn. Just heat. His hands are everywhere, his mouth on mine, and my head is spinning. He tastes like whiskey and desire. I can't breathe and don't want to.

We move together in the dark, shedding layers and navigating by touch and urgency. I don't think. I just want to feel something that doesn't ache.

And with Ethan, I do.

Right now, I want to be wanted. And he wants me.

So I let him.

Chapter 9

Grayson

I don't know why I'm watching them.

The second a guy slides onto the stool beside Maddie, I recognize him from the photo on her phone last week—Ethan. The doctor. The one she's been texting late at night, smiling like he invented oxygen. My stomach twists into a knot I can't untangle. My grip tightens around the glass in my hand as I take another drink; the whiskey burns uselessly against the heat building in my chest. She's smiling at him, leaning in slightly, just enough to be intimate. He says something, and she laughs, tipping her head back, and I feel that laugh like a punch to the ribs.

Why the fuck do I care?

I shouldn't. I don't.

But I don't look away.

The music's bass pulses through my chest, a steady heartbeat matching the anger simmering beneath my skin. It's not the music I'm focused on though, it's them.

Ethan reaches for Maddie's hand, and she lets him pull her onto the dance floor. My fingers clench around my glass as I watch his hands settle possessively on her waist, pulling her in until there's no space left. She's looking up at him, her lips moving, talking? Flirting? I can't hear anything, but I don't need to.

I see it all.

The way he leans in, murmuring something against her ear. She smiles, soft and breathless, her cheeks flushed in a way I've never seen directed at me. The way her fingers curl into his shirt, steadying herself against him like she's dizzy with his attention. My chest tightens further, heat crawling up my neck. Jealousy coils around my lungs until it's hard to breathe.

She met him last year, back when we played here. I remember her mentioning he was a doctor, a pediatrician, some guy she ran into when we were in town. I hadn't thought much of it then. But now, seeing his hand drift lower, pulling her flush against him?

I want to put my fist through something.

I slam my glass down harder than intended, whiskey splashing over the edge. A few heads turn, but I ignore them. My pulse is hammering, my jaw clenched so tight it aches.

I don't know what I expected. Maddie is free to do whatever she wants; it's not my business.

Except it feels like it is.

I'm on my third drink, maybe my fourth, when they make their way toward the door. Maddie says something, smiling shyly, and Ethan's hand slides confidently lower, guiding her out of the bar like she belongs to him. My muscles coil, and I'm halfway out of my seat before I realize what I'm doing.

Then Jensen steps in front of me.

"Sit back down."

I shake my head, trying to step around him, but he doesn't budge. His eyes narrow.

"Don't be an idiot, Grayson."

I exhale sharply, signing too fast, frustration bleeding into every gesture. ***"You don't even know what's going on."***

"I know enough." Jensen crosses his arms, steady as always. ***"You've been watching her all night like you're about to start a fight, and now you're going to chase after her? What exactly are you planning to do?"***

I open my mouth, then snap it shut. I don't fucking know.

Jensen sighs, rubbing a hand over his face before signing slowly, pointedly. ***"Maddie works for us. For you. That makes this unbalanced. You get that, right?"***

I grit my teeth. ***"She's not..."***

"She is." He cuts me off, his expression hard. *"You're famous. She's our PA. The power dynamic is there even if you don't see it."*

I huff out a breath, shaking my head. *"Ethan isn't any better."*

Jensen raises an eyebrow, skeptical. *"And why's that?"*

"We don't know him."

"He's a pediatrician, not a damn arms dealer."

I scowl. *"Doctors can be assholes too."*

Jensen's expression doesn't change. *"And musicians can't?"*

That one lands like a blow. My hands still. My pulse thrums, hard and painful.

Jensen doesn't let up. *"Maddie's watched you for months, you know. She's seen you take groupies back to your room. She knows exactly how this ends."*

My stomach knots. *"That's different."*

"How?"

I don't have an answer. All the arguments die on my fingers.

Jensen exhales through his nose, watching me closely. *"You don't get to be mad, Grayson. You have no right to be mad."*

His words hit harder than I want to admit. I swallow the retort burning in my brain, my hands flexing uselessly at my sides. Maddie's gone. Out the door. With him.

Jensen waits, watching me carefully. I don't sign anything else. I sink back into my chair, grabbing my drink again with too much force.

Jensen nods once.

And then he sits beside me, not saying anything at all.

I don't know how long I've been sitting here, nursing drinks, eyes fixed on the door as if Maddie might walk back in any second.

She doesn't.

I shouldn't care. I tell myself I don't. But every time the door swings open, my gaze snaps up, my stomach tightens, and disappointment sinks deeper each time it's not her. She left with him. That's all that matters.

I finish my whiskey, the burn useless against the ache in my chest.

A movement catches my eye—a flash of blonde hair and red lips. A hand lands on my thigh, fingers trailing upward, teasing. When I turn, she's already watching me. Blue eyes, heavy-lidded, a practiced seductive smile. She leans in, lips forming words I don't bother trying to read. She doesn't care if I understand her. Instead, she lifts her hand, pinching a tiny baggie between her fingers.

White pills.

I arch an eyebrow, and she grins wider. Her fingers brush my jaw, tilting my face toward hers. She lifts a single pill, pressing it gently to my lips.

"Open," she mouths slowly.

I let her slip it onto my tongue. Her mouth seals over mine, her tongue sweeping against mine as the pill dissolves bitterly. I swallow, chasing the taste of whiskey and regret with her kiss.

The world shifts abruptly.

Lights blur, halos of gold and red streak through the haze. The bass throbs beneath my skin, pulsing like a second heartbeat.

She's laughing, her body pressed insistently against mine. Another girl joins—brunette, eyes dark, curious, and hungry.

I don't stop them.

I don't stop any of it.

The next thing I know, we're stumbling into my hotel room.

The blonde shoves me onto the bed, straddling me as she rocks her hips. Her lips part in silent pleasure, hands raking down my chest.

Heat. Skin. Mouths. Hands.

The brunette joins, lips trailing across my throat, fingers sliding down my torso.

My head lolls back as the drug takes hold; every touch is electric and overwhelming.

I let go.

I let them pull me under, chasing a high that has nothing to do with the pill dissolving in my bloodstream.

For a while, I don't think.

For a while, I forget.

Chapter 10
Maddie

The scent of coffee and fresh pastries wraps around me like a comforting embrace as I sink back into my chair, sighing contentedly. Morning sunlight filters gently through the window in the hotel's café , illuminating the golden flakes scattered from the croissant I just tore apart.

Across from me, Ethan watches with an easy grin, fingers tracing lazy patterns along the rim of his coffee cup. "Good night?" he asks teasingly, taking a sip.

I arch an eyebrow, lips quirking upward. "Decent."

He sputters on his coffee, laughter bright in his eyes. "Decent? That's all I get?"

Smirking, I pop another piece of croissant into my mouth. "Fine. Maybe better than decent."

He leans closer, voice dropping to a husky murmur. "You were making some pretty compelling arguments for spectacular last night."

Heat rushes up my neck, but before I can reply, a familiar voice interrupts.

"Maddie, have you seen Grayson?"

Delilah stands beside our table, arms crossed, a frown creasing her features.

I blink in surprise. "Uh... not since Jake's last night. Why?"

She huffs, annoyance edging her voice. "He's not answering his phone. I even rang the flashing doorbell in his room, but nothing."

That's odd. Grayson isn't exactly easy to rouse, but he always reacts to the doorbell's flash.

I glance at my watch—past ten already. And I didn't spot him at breakfast.

That's even stranger. Grayson never misses the hotel's complimentary breakfasts. Ever.

"I can check on him after breakfast," I offer, brushing crumbs from my fingertips.

Delilah sighs, nodding stiffly. "Thanks. And if he's still asleep in an hour, pour ice water on him for me."

Ethan's phone buzzes against the table, and his relaxed expression shifts, urgency flickering across his face.

"Emergency at the hospital—I have to go."

He rises swiftly, pulling out his wallet to toss a cash tip onto the table. Before I can respond, he cups my face gently, kissing me deeply, lingering just enough to leave me breathless.

"See you later?" he whispers against my lips.

"Go save lives, doc," I say softly, smiling despite my disappointment.

He grins, gently squeezing my shoulder before disappearing swiftly out the door.

Delilah watches him leave, her gaze flicking mischievously back to me. "Well, someone had a good night."

"Nosy," I retort, sipping my coffee and trying to hide my blush.

"Not nosy. Observant," she counters smoothly, stealing the last bite of my croissant. "And that man looks at you like he'd rather have you for breakfast."

I nearly choke, warmth flooding my face as Delilah cackles gleefully.

I drain the last of my coffee, pushing away from the table. "Alright, let me go deal with your problem child."

"Good luck," she calls after me, eyes sparkling wickedly.

I head to the front desk, offering a sweet smile as I request a key to Grayson's room for a welfare check. The staff knows our routine, handing me a card without question.

My stomach knots slightly as the elevator climbs to his floor. Standing before his door, I knock firmly, then trigger the flashing doorbell. Nothing.

Exhaling sharply, I swipe the keycard and step inside.

The smell hits me first: sour booze, stale sweat, and something more intimate, more invasive. My gut churns uneasily.

The room is a disaster: empty bottles are scattered across surfaces, glasses are stacked carelessly, and clothing, including someone's dress from last night, litters the carpet.

My heart pounds uncomfortably as I step further inside. When the bed comes into view, nausea rolls through me.

Grayson lies sprawled across the mattress, arm thrown over his face, lost between two women, very much naked beneath tangled sheets. A blonde curls possessively into his side, fingers brushing lazily across his bare stomach. A brunette's legs twine around his, intimately comfortable.

Bile rises sharply. My throat constricts painfully. Not my business, I tell myself. It shouldn't matter. Yet my eyes catch on something else: a purse on the floor, a clear baggie protruding with tiny white pills.

My breath stalls. I kneel, fingers hovering over the bag. There's no proof. No certainty Grayson took anything. It might not even belong to him. But my mind races and doubt creeps like ice beneath my skin. Shaking my head sharply, I stand quickly. This isn't my mess. I grab my phone and text Delilah.

Me: *He's sleeping off a bender with two new friends.*

Her reply is immediate, vibrating angrily in my hand.

Delilah: *Are you fucking kidding me? I'll kill him. His funeral is Thursday.*

I silence my phone as it buzzes angrily again. I don't tell her about the pills. I back quietly out of the room, pulling the door shut with careful detachment. I try not to think about why it stings so sharply. I don't answer Delilah's furious texts. Not immediately. Not in the elevator. Not even when the bustling lobby noise crashes into me.

Instead, I head outside, the crisp morning air stinging my skin. The loading area is quiet and deserted. I sink onto the curb, resting my elbows on my knees, staring unseeingly at the pavement. I'm not crying. Not angry. Just... empty. It shouldn't matter. Whatever Grayson does with his body, with those women, isn't my concern. But seeing it firsthand, something inside me splintered—something fragile and dangerous I hadn't let myself name.

I rub tiredly at my eyes, pulling my phone from my pocket. My thumb hovers over the message thread I opened earlier—

Ethan.

He kissed me goodbye. Said he had to run—a hospital emergency. I shouldn't bother him. But still, for a second, I think about it. Think about how easy it would be to text *anything* just to feel wanted. Just to feel... something. Instead, I lock the screen and press the phone to my chest. My heart feels tight. Suffocating.

I need a moment. Just one. A reminder of why I'm here. Why I took this job.

It's work.

He's just work.

This whole thing is just a job.

Inhaling slowly, I push up from the curb and slip back inside, finding an empty hallway near catering. I lean against the cool wall, letting solitude wrap around me.

I just need a moment alone.

Chapter 11

Grayson

My head splits open in agony, sharp and relentless, like someone's driving an ice pick through my skull. The instant I move, my stomach protests violently, a sour taste rising to coat my throat. My limbs feel disconnected, heavy, and useless, as if someone dragged me across concrete and left me to rot. I force my eyes open, immediately regretting it as sunlight sears into my skull. My vision swims, the edges blurred by pain, my mouth parched. The sheets beside me are rumpled, reeking of stale perfume, sweat, and sex. The women from last night are gone.

Good.

I roll to my back, stomach lurching in rebellion, and throw an arm across my eyes to block the stabbing daylight. My phone buzzes insistently from the nightstand, vibrating sharply against the wood. I ignore it. It buzzes again. And again. Grimacing, I grab it, nearly fumbling the damn thing. The screen blurs, then clears.

Delilah. Jensen. Maddie.

I sit up too quickly, biting back nausea as dizziness slams into me. My fingers shake as I scroll through messages.

Delilah: *Are you alive?*

Me: *Barely.*

Delilah: *No, are you fucking stupid?*

I groan, forcing my aching body upright and staggering toward the bathroom.

Me: *What now?*

Delilah: *Really? After last night's shitshow? I had to send Maddie to check if you were breathing this morning.*

I freeze, my grip tightening painfully around the phone.

Maddie saw me like this?

Me: *When?*

Delilah: *This morning. Why?*

I exhale shakily, bracing myself against the bathroom counter, my reflection haunted and haggard. The room was a mess, the bottles and clothes everywhere, the lingering evidence of debauchery painfully obvious.

Shit.

Me: *I'm fine. Calm down.*

Delilah: *Oh, sure. CALM DOWN because you're fine after waking up in bed with two random women?*

I snort bitterly, heading back into the room to dig through my duffel bag for clean clothes.

Me: *You've had your share of nights, D.*

Delilah: *At least I've never woken up next to strangers.*

That one hits harder than it should. My jaw tightens. My chest aches.

Me: *So what? I'm not dating anyone.*

Delilah: *Right. That makes everything okay.*

I mute my phone, throwing it onto the bed. I already feel like shit. I don't need Delilah's judgment piled on top. The shower is scalding, steam filling my lungs and slowly clearing my head. Still, thoughts linger stubbornly. Maddie saw everything. My gut twists painfully. How long did she stand there, taking it all in? The empty bottles, discarded clothes, the naked women? My jaw clenches again. If she saw, she wouldn't say anything. Maddie doesn't do confrontations. She locks it down tight and holds everything inside, even when it hurts her.

But I notice.

I always notice.

I rest my forehead against the cool tile, inhaling deeply, willing the tension to ease. Yet, another image crashes through, bright and uninvited, Maddie last night, eyes sparkling behind her glasses, laughing at something Ethan whispered. My fists clench against the slick wall.

She was breathtaking. Effortlessly sexy. I couldn't look away.

And now I imagine her here, pressed against me under the steaming water, her fingers dragging over my skin, her lips on my throat. Heat surges through my veins, frustration coiling tightly in my chest.

Fuck.

I push the thought away harshly, stepping out to dry off. I shouldn't think of Maddie after what she saw or last night's disaster. But my mind refuses to let her go.

It's always her.

By the time I dress and head downstairs, the headache is manageable, though exhaustion drags at my limbs. Sunglasses shield me from harsh daylight as I slip into the hotel restaurant, craving coffee and the relief it might offer. The restaurant is too much at first, but I push through it. I pick a quiet booth, dropping heavily into the seat. The waitress that approaches is blonde, her shirt strategically low. Her smile falters slightly when I signal I'm deaf, but she quickly scribbles her greeting on the pad.

What can I get you, sweetheart?

I jot down my order, coffee underlined twice. She smiles flirtatiously, but I barely register her as she moves away. My stomach twists uneasily. I glance out the window, the afternoon sun making everything feel too real.

When I glance up again, Maddie is there. She stands hesitantly across the room, arms wrapped tightly around herself. Our eyes meet, tension crackling through the distance. Then, determinedly, she moves toward me, sliding into the booth opposite.

My heart rate spikes.

She sets her phone down firmly between us, hands moving briskly. *"We've been touring for three years."*

I arch an eyebrow, feigning nonchalance. *"Your point?"*

"A lot of bands spiral at this point. Partying gets intense. It burns people out."

I huff a laugh, smirking humorlessly. *"You sleep with one doctor, and now you're my therapist?"*

Maddie recoils, eyes flaring. *"Are you seriously that much of an asshole?"*

"Maybe," I sign sharply. *"Ask your boyfriend. Is he your boyfriend, Maddie, or another guy who wants you because you're with Wild Child Reckless?"*

Her eyes flash dangerously, fingers flying. *"You're a hypocrite. Do you realize I've often ignored you bringing random groupies to your room? How many nights have I pretended not to care? At least Ethan genuinely cares about me, unlike anyone you've ever touched."*

Each word lands with bruising force. My stomach churns with shame, my fists tightening against my thighs. And still, memories flicker of her silent support every time she brought me tea without being asked, remembered my favorite snack, and smoothed out the chaos I created. She was always behind the scenes, always steady, always there. She waits, shoulders trembling with barely contained anger, daring me to respond.

But I have nothing. No defense. She's right, and the truth scorches deep.

I stare at the table, silent, unable to look at her. After a moment, Maddie exhales sharply, pushing herself from the booth, her eyes hard with disappointment. Without another word, she walks away, leaving me alone with my self-inflicted wounds. The waitress returns with coffee I no longer want.

I don't stop her from setting it down. I don't even glance her way.

I just sit there.

I feel every broken part of myself echoing in the silence she left behind.

Chapter 12
Maddie

I stare at him from across the table, barely restraining the urge to strangle him.

Delilah was right. He might die today.

Grayson fucking Stone lounges in his booth like he doesn't have a care in the world. Sunglasses shield whatever mess is behind them. The usual cocky smirk is gone, but he still tries to act like he's in control.

He isn't.

I grip my phone tighter, my heart pounding with frustration and worry. He shifts in his seat, casual to the point of being infuriating—like I'm overreacting.

I exhale sharply, forcing myself to stay calm. ***"I saw the pills, Grayson."***

His fingers twitch, his jaw tightening, but his expression doesn't change. ***"You don't know what you're talking about."***

"I know exactly what I saw."

He scoffs, shaking his head. ***"Relax, Maddie. You only care because it's your job."***

That lands like a slap, sharp and stinging. I swallow the lump in my throat, my hands curling into fists. My vision blurs at the edges, but I blink it away. Three years. After all the time we've spent together, after everything I've done for him, does he still think this is just a job? After that Denver show, I stayed up with him when he was shaking so hard he couldn't hold down water. I called his mom because he couldn't, and I held the damn bucket while he puked. But sure, I only care because it's my job.

For a second, I consider walking out. Letting him sit there in his own mess. But something inside me cracks. I shove to my feet and slam my palms on the table. The sound rings out, sharp and jarring. A few heads turn, but I don't care.

"I care more than just for my job." My voice wavers as the anger spills out. ***"You need to listen to me, Grayson. I know what I saw and where this path ends."***

His jaw tightens. He sips his coffee, pretending he's unaffected. ***"You're overreacting."***

I shake my head, the anger draining into something heavier. ***"Call your mom."***

His brow furrows. ***"I always call her at noon on Sundays."***

I take a slow breath and meet his gaze, letting the weight of my words settle. ***"It's two o'clock, Grayson."***

He stiffens. His posture shifts.

I don't stop. ***"She already texted me."***

His grip tightens around the mug. He doesn't speak. Doesn't move. Out of the corner of my eye, I catch Jensen across the room, watching with that quiet stillness that means he knows exactly how bad this is. He doesn't move. Doesn't interrupt. Just watches.

And I don't wait. I turn and walk out, leaving Grayson behind. The elevator doors close, and I sag back against the metal wall, my hands still trembling. The adrenaline is fading, leaving my thoughts scrambled and raw. I shouldn't care this much. But I do. My phone buzzes in my pocket. I pull it out, expecting Delilah or maybe even his mom.

It's him.

Grayson: *I called her.*

Just three words. No excuses. No jokes.

I let out a breath, slow and shaky. It's a start. The elevator dings, and I step out. My feet carry me down the hallway toward my room, but my mind spins. I want to tell Delilah. To talk it out. But then I think of her stumbling in drunk, laughing like nothing mattered. She's not in a place to give advice. And if I say this out loud, if I admit what I'm seeing—that Grayson is slipping—it becomes real.

By the time I reach my room, my head pounds. I shut the door and lean back against it, pressing my palms over my face.

My phone buzzes.

Delilah: *Did you kill him, or do I need to book a casket?*

I don't answer. Not yet. Not until I know how bad this really is. Then I reach for my phone again.

Me: *We need to talk about the band.*

Cora replies fast.

Cora: *What's going on?*

I hesitate. I can't give her everything. Not yet. Not while trying to protect Grayson. But I can't lie either.

Me: *They're exhausted. We need to slow down. Head back to LA. Just take a break.*

A long pause.

Cora: *I've been worried too. You're not the first to bring it up.*

My chest tightens.

Me: *Who else?*

Cora: *Patrick. Even Jensen has been quiet lately.*

That makes me go still. Jensen is the rock. The one who never cracks.

Me: *Can we do something?*

Cora: *Let me make some calls. I'll keep you posted.*

It's not a fix, but it's something. I drop the phone onto the bed and press the heels of my hands to my eyes. Something has to give. Because if it doesn't, this band is going to fall apart. And I don't know who will go first. Grayson. Or me. I cross to the window and pull the curtain aside. The street below bustles with people who have no idea something is unraveling just a few floors above them.

My phone buzzes again.

One new message. Grayson. I stare at the screen, breath caught.

Grayson: *I'm trying.*

Just two words. But I don't think they're a performance. They're not part of his usual routine.

Maybe they're real.

I press the phone to my chest momentarily and let myself believe him. Then I close my eyes and rest my forehead against the cool glass. Tomorrow, we start again. Another city. Another show. Another storm quietly brewing. And maybe, if he says something honest again, I won't have to walk away.

Chapter 13

Grayson

My phone buzzes once against the table. I glance at the screen.

Maddie: *Can we talk?*

No emoji. Just plain and direct, like always. I don't answer. I don't even have time. She's already walking toward me. Clipboard gone. Hair up. Shoulders set in that way that says this isn't a work thing. I stiffen as she slides into the booth across from me. Her movements are careful, deliberate. Her eyes scan my face—what little she can see behind the sunglasses I haven't taken off all morning.

She doesn't waste time.

Her hands move in that precise, controlled way that makes my chest hurt.

"I saw your message. If you meant it—we need to talk."

I shift in my seat. The coffee in front of me is still full. Untouched.

Her hands stay low, fingers tightening. Then she signs again, slower now:

"You don't have to explain everything. But you need to figure out what you're doing. With the band. With... this."

She looks at me like she's waiting. For anything. A flinch. A sign. A hint that I've heard her. I don't move. I could say something. I could sign the truth: That I'm trying. That I'm scared. That it's not just her I'm letting down—it's everyone.

But my hands stay still. Her shoulders drop slightly, the smallest deflation.

"Don't expect me to keep pretending it's fine."

And then she gets up and walks out.

I don't follow her. I sit there long after Maddie's gone, the last of my coffee gone cold between my hands. Her words won't stop circling. The way she looked at me—furious, disappointed, hurt.

She's right. And I hate that.

* * *

By the time I drag myself out of the booth and head back to the venue, the hallway's already alive with crew and gear cases. I'm not looking for anyone. Just space.

But Delilah finds me.

She's posted up near the catering table, donut in one hand, her other tapping a brutal rhythm into her phone screen. The second she spots me, she lifts a brow like she's been waiting for round two.

I sign a stiff *"Hey."*

Delilah doesn't bother with pleasantries. She scoffs and signs, **"You were supposed to be up an hour ago."**

I shrug, jaw tight. *"Why'd you send Maddie?"*

She lifts a brow.

"I figured you'd be less of an ass to her than anyone else."

I shake my head. *"She didn't say anything when she was in my room."*

Delilah's hands move fast, biting. *"Because she's Maddie. She found you passed out, room reeking of booze and perfume, and instead of losing it, she just handled it. Like she always does."*

I look away.

"She texted me after," Delilah adds, her expression hard. *"Said you were breathing. That's it."*

Then, with a bitter scoff, *"She didn't even mention the half-dressed circus she walked in on either. Guess even she has limits."*

My chest tightens.

I knew Maddie had come by—I just didn't realize she was the one who found me like *that*. ***"I didn't ask her to go."***

"No, you didn't. You just made it her job to clean up after you." The words land hard.

Delilah takes a breath, then folds her arms. ***"She was outside after breakfast. Near the loading dock. I went to get coffee and saw her on the phone, pacing."***

I glance at her. ***"And?"***

"She said something about sending money. Sounded tense. Maybe she's got bills. Family stuff. Whatever it was, it didn't sound casual."

"Money for what?"

Delilah shrugs. ***"How should I know? I didn't stand there and eavesdrop. But you might want to check your ego. Just because she's good at her job doesn't mean she's not struggling."***

The jab lands square in my chest. **"I'll *find Jensen.*"**

"Yeah," she says, popping the rest of her donut in her mouth. ***"You do that."***

I take the long way toward the back of the venue and spot Maddie in the hallway, sitting on a flight case. She's curled inward, phone in her hands, thumb flying across the screen, eyes tight with focus. She doesn't look up.

I stop. And I turn the other way.

Jensen's over by the board, plugging something in. He looks up. *"You alive?"*

I sign, *"Have you noticed anything off with Maddie lately?"*

He blinks. *"Off how?"*

"Like... stressed. Hiding something."

He shrugs. *"She always looks like she's carrying ten people's weight, but nah—nothing out of the ordinary. Why?"*

I hesitate. *"Just wondering."*

He nods, unconcerned, and goes back to his work. But I can't shake it. If Maddie's sending money home... if she *really needs this job*, then what the hell am I doing? I can't be the thing that makes her life harder. I can't drag her into my mess because I'm too selfish to ignore my feelings. She deserves more than that. Even if it kills me to walk away.

The stage lights are blinding. The crowd's a blur—just motion and energy pulsing under my feet—but I see her.

Maddie.

Off to the side, clipboard in hand, headset resting behind one ear, eyes glued to the stage. She's pacing, her shoulders tight, one hand rubbing the back of her neck like she's holding this whole show together with sheer force of will. And maybe she is. I miss a visual cue—late on a shift—and Jensen glances at me, eyes sharp. I snap back into it, catching the rhythm again, slamming into the beat. But I keep looking at her. Every few seconds. She doesn't look at me once. Her jaw's tight. Her posture wound like a wire.

Something's wrong.

Or maybe everything's wrong and I'm just now noticing it. Too late. By the time we finish the set, I'm soaked in sweat, my hands still buzzing from the drums. I climb down from the riser and grab a towel, wiping my face, but my eyes don't leave the edge of the stage.

Maddie's gone.

Jensen appears beside me and gives a quick thumbs-up. I nod back, but I'm already scanning the exit. I spot her through the side curtain—out in the hallway, back turned, phone to her ear. Her hand gestures sharply as she walks, fast and focused. She disappears around the corner before I can move. Something's eating at her. And I don't know if it's *me*. Probably *because* of me. I grab a bottle of water and head backstage, ready to find her, to ask—to *do* something. But then I feel someone else—familiar presence, familiar weight.

Delilah.

She's leaning against the wall near the gear crates, arms folded, her expression sharper than usual. There's a drink in her hand, but it's barely touched. Her eyes are on me, steady and unblinking.

She signs, ***"If you're looking for Maddie, give her some space."***

I lift a brow, defensive before I mean to be.

Delilah's mouth presses into a tight line before she signs again, slower this time. ***"She's pissed. And hurt. And I get it."***

I don't answer. She steps closer, lowering the drink to her side.

"You scared her, Gray." That lands harder than anything else could.

"I know you didn't mean to. I know you're trying to keep it together. But she's not just holding you up out there. She's holding all of us."

I look away, jaw tight.

Delilah sighs, her shoulders dropping a fraction. Her tone softens even as her hands stay firm. ***"She's asking questions. About LA. About time off."*** She pauses. ***"She's figuring out her limits. We all are."***

I nod once, slowly. I feel it in my chest more than anywhere else.

Delilah looks at me with equal parts annoyance and affection and signs: ***"You don't have to be perfect. But you can't keep making her clean it up."***

I nod again, but she's already turning, already walking away. And I'm left standing there, the truth sitting heavy in my chest.

Chapter 14
Maddie

The hallway is colder than I expect, like the hotel's air conditioning is trying to keep me from feeling anything. I keep walking. Past the elevator. Past the lobby. Past the tight feeling in my chest that won't unclench no matter how often I tell myself I'm fine.

I'm not.

My fingers are still curled from where I clenched them at the table. My throat is raw from words I didn't say—ones I swallowed because saying them out loud would've made it too real. Grayson didn't deny the pills. He just deflected and acted like I didn't care. Like I was nothing more than a clipboard in human form. A flicker of movement pulls my attention—one of the front desk clerks raising a hand, a small box balanced in the other.

"Miss Maddie?"

I blink. "Uh... yeah?"

He offers it with a polite smile, the kind that's too practiced to be personal. "This was just delivered. No card—just a tag with your name." I murmur a thank you and take it from him, the weight of it oddly grounding in my hands. It's neatly wrapped—brown paper and gold ribbon—and carefully so, like someone took their time. I pull the ribbon free and lift the lid. Inside is a slim white envelope and a small black velvet box. My heart thumps once, hard.

I open the envelope.

Thought you could use a reason to smile today. I'd love to see you tonight if you're not too busy saving the band.

—E

Ethan.

Of course it's Ethan. I open the box. Four deep red roses lie inside, trimmed and arranged in a silver-lined tray, the petals soft and perfect. Romantic, thoughtful, not over-the-top, just *nice*. Tears prick at the backs of my eyes before I can stop them. He's the kind of man who sends flowers without a reason, who remembers what color nail polish I wore three weeks ago, and who listens when I vent about how long load-ins take. He has soft edges and warm safety. And for a second, I ache to want that more than I do. I touch one of the petals. It's impossibly smooth. Beautiful. Simple. But when I close the box and tuck it under my arm, all I can think about is how Grayson looked this morning—wild-eyed and wrecked. Lost in his own mess. He didn't even realize I was there until it was too late.

And even then, he still tried to push me away. Ethan is flowers, gentle touches, and predictability.

Grayson is chaos, silence, and heat. And for reasons I can't justify, it's the latter I can't stop thinking about.

Two days later — Cincinnati

The concert is a blur of flashing lights and moving bodies. I'm backstage most of the time, barking into my headset, adjusting schedules on the fly, and trying to stay ahead of every potential disaster. One of the drum triggers shorts out during soundcheck. Jensen's wireless rig glitches mid-song. A vendor no-shows, and I have to scramble to shift the catering order.

I don't stop moving. I don't let myself stop. But every time I glance at the stage, I see him.

Grayson.

He's locked in. Shirt clinging to him with sweat, muscles flexing as he slams the beat into submission. On the outside, he looks fine. In control. Electric. But I know better. I see the cracks. The way his gaze keeps sliding to me between songs. The tension in his shoulders that has nothing to do with the tempo.

He's watching me.

Trying to figure out if I'm still angry. If I'm about to walk. And the worst part? I don't even know the answer myself. After the encore, when the lights go down and the house starts clearing, I'm gone. I duck through the service hallway and into the night air, tugging my jacket tighter around myself. The venue's noise fades behind me, replaced by the hum of the city. I pull out my phone and hit dial. Not Ethan. Not Cora. Just someone who might listen. Mom's voice comes over the line full of concern.

"Yeah, I'm still thinking about it. No, no. I'm okay. I'm just... tired. It's been a lot." I sigh. "I don't know. Maybe it's time. Maybe I just need to breathe for a while."

I keep my voice even. Detached. I don't say the part about Grayson. I won't say how scared I am that he won't even ask me to stay if I leave. When I hang up, I don't feel better. Just... hollow. I go back through the side entrance, keeping my head down, hoping no one sees me.

"Hey."

Delilah's voice cuts through the backstage hallway like a whip. I look up, startled. She's leaning over the second-floor landing above the catering table, drink in hand, watching me like she's already read my mind. Her gaze flicks to the roses tucked under my arm, and something shifts behind her eyes; something I can't quite name. I offer a tight nod and keep walking. The elevator ride feels endless. When I step into my room, I set the roses on the desk and sink onto the bed, my jacket still on, the adrenaline fading.

I could have something else. Something easy. Something stable and uncomplicated and safe. But every time I try to picture a future with Ethan, I see Grayson instead—furious, grieving, aching in silence. And somewhere deep down, I think... maybe I don't want easy. I just want someone who sees me.

Even when I'm breaking.

Chapter 15

Grayson

This is our last show in Portland, and Delilah is ready to show up and party hard once the Little Whiskey Girl tour is over. Mom will want me to come home, but I am just not ready. I've signed up to be a guest drummer with a local group in L.A.- Black Hollow.

It's a temporary local gig, but they're big in the scene. It's good exposure, a challenge, and a way to keep my hands busy and my mind from drifting. When Mom calls, I already know what she's going to say. I rub my temples as I answer, and the video call connects. Her face fills the screen, familiar and warm, but there's worry in her eyes. She's sitting at the kitchen table where I used to do my homework. The light from the window makes her look softer, like she's part of the past, something I can almost touch but not quite reach.

"Grayson, you need to come home."

I shift, bracing myself. I already feel the pull of home, but I push it aside. This chance, this moment, could change everything. I need to prove that I'm more than just a guy in a band. *"I can't, Mom. I took a guest spot with another band, and it's a big deal."*

Her fingers hesitate mid-sign, her expression tightening. She knows what this means—I know she does—but she's still a mother who wants her youngest child close. Especially since I'm the one who left. The one who's farthest away. *"You haven't been home in over a year. Your sisters are here, and you're not. You know how much your father and I miss you."*

I shake my head, fingers moving quickly. *"It's not about them, Mom. I need to do this. It's my chance."*

She pauses, watching me, her eyes soft but sad. *"I don't understand why you can't come home, even briefly. Jensen and Delilah are talking about coming back. Why not you?"*

The words hit harder than I expect. Jensen and Delilah. They don't understand either. They don't know what it's like to feel like you don't belong in one place and your purpose is elsewhere. Besides, Delilah is wrapped up in Alexander, and Jensen tries to drink Lily's memory away every day.

"It's not the same, Mom." My signing is sharp, and my emotions are tangled in the movements. *"I need to keep pushing. I can't go back—not yet."*

She studies me for a long moment. Then, finally, her hands move again, slower this time. ***"I don't want to lose you."***

My breath catches. ***"I'm not leaving you, Mom. I just need to find my own way."***

Her hands tremble slightly as she signs, her expression filled with something I don't want to name. ***"I know you need to do this. I just wish I could hold you and tell you it'll be okay."***

My throat tightens. ***"I know. I miss you too."***

The silence stretches between us, filled with everything we're not saying. Finally, she signs one last time, slow and soft. ***"Promise me you'll take care of yourself?"***

I nod, even though I know this is a promise I can't fully keep. But I will try. I will, for her. ***"I promise, Mom."***

She smiles, but it's sad, and I feel it deep in my chest. ***"I love you, Grayson."***

"I love you too." And then the call ends, leaving me in the quiet room, my heart heavy.

The club is alive with a pulsing heartbeat of bass and flashing lights. The air is thick with sweat, smoke, and something electric, something untamed. After the set, the guys from Black Hollow drag me along, pulling me into their world. The music is so loud it could rattle the teeth out of my head, but all I feel is the deep vibrations rolling through my chest, shaking my bones. Bodies press together on the dance floor, a writhing mass of movement and sound. The energy is infectious and wild. I stay near the back, letting it wash over me, feeling the thud of the bass in my veins. A heavy weight drops onto the seat next to me. The bassist, Wes, slides a shot across the table before throwing one back himself. His grin is lopsided, eyes glazed but still sharp.

"Drink up, man," he mouths, though I don't need to read his lips to understand. I take the shot, the burn spreading through my chest, grounding me in the chaos.

Across from me, the lead singer, Knox, leans forward, rubbing a hand under his nose before sliding a tray toward Wes. There's an unspoken exchange, a rhythm between them, something practiced and easy. I hesitate when Wes passes it to me, but only for a second. I don't think about what it is. I think about the way my pulse pounds in my throat, the way the world blurs at the edges, the way the music becomes something I can almost feel beyond my skin. The moment stretches, weightless and infinite, and my mind is quiet for once.

I let it take me under.

I surface, but it's like swimming through molasses. My limbs feel heavy and disconnected like they belong to someone else. My head tilts back against the pillow, and my vision sharpens and blurs in turns.

There's a woman on top of me. I don't recognize her. Her movements are slow and unfocused as she rides me. The glow of neon filters in from some unseen source, painting her in shifting hues of blue and purple. I blink, trying to piece together how I got here, but the memories slip away like water through my fingers. Other couples move in a slow, hazy rhythm around the room. Shadows stretch long across the walls, bodies tangled in a dance that somehow feels intimate and detached. The air is thick and heavy with something I can't name.

I should leave.

The thought drifts through my mind, faint and distant, but before I can grasp it—before I can move—I slip under again.

I wake to silence. The air is stale, thick with sweat, and something acrid. My head pounds, my mouth dry as I push myself upright. The room is empty now, with nothing but scattered mattresses and the ghosts of what happened here. My stomach twists. My skin feels too tight, too hot. I find my pants in a heap nearby. My wallet is still there, but it's empty. My phone—thank God—is still in my pocket. I clutch it like a lifeline as I stumble toward the door, stepping over discarded bottles and crumpled clothes.

I don't know where I am. Portland, yeah, but not any part I recognize. The Uber ride back to the hotel is long. The city rolls past in a blur of neon and darkened windows, and all I can think about is the ache in my chest and the way my hands shake when I press them together. When I step into my room, I head straight for the shower. The water scalds, but I let it. I scrub at my skin, trying to wash away everything I don't remember.

When I step out, my phone buzzes. A text from Knox.

Knox: *Are you in for tonight?*

I hesitate, just for a second.

Then I type back.

Me: *Yeah. See you there.*

Chapter 16

Maddie

I step into the hotel lobby, gripping the keycard so tightly that my fingers start to ache. Grayson hasn't answered my texts or called back in days, and when I checked in with him last week, his responses were strange, like he was pulling further away. I've tried to give him space, but I can't help this nagging worry clawing at me. It's been six weeks. I should've come sooner.

I know it's none of my business, but I can't shake the feeling that something isn't right. I wait as the elevator ascends, the little ping echoing in the silence. My thoughts are tangled up in him, in everything I don't understand about his life, about how I could be so close to someone but still feel like there's so much I don't know. Grayson's world is quiet in a way that I can't even imagine. I wish I could crawl inside his head and feel the world like he does. I hate that sometimes. I feel like I'm on the outside looking in.

I take a deep breath when the elevator doors open to his floor. His room is just ahead. 12-23. I ring the doorbell, the flashing light flickering in the dim hall. There's no answer. I wait a moment longer, my fingers fidgeting at my side, before I slide the keycard through the lock. The door clicks open, and I step inside.

The room is quieter than I expect. Too quiet. The mess hits me first. Clothes are tossed carelessly across the floor, empty bottles litter the furniture, and I can smell something stale. It's the kind of chaos that comes from a night—or maybe several—of partying, of losing control. I swallow down the tightness in my chest, wishing I didn't feel like I already know what I'm about to find.

And then I see him.

Grayson is passed out on the bed, sprawled awkwardly, his arm hanging off the side of the mattress. His breathing is shallow but steady. I just watch him for a moment, unsure whether to wake him or let him sleep. But then I notice something. A sharp pang hits my chest as I take in the mirrors scattered around the room. They're the last thing I expected. I don't know why they glint in the dim light, but they make everything feel worse. A part of me wants to look away. To pretend I didn't see them. But I can't.

I walk toward the bed, kneeling beside him. His face turns into the pillow, his hair messy and sweaty. He doesn't stir when

I gently shake his shoulder. Grayson's body feels tense under my touch as if it is holding something back.

I shake his shoulder. He doesn't move. I try again, harder. Nothing.

A heavy sigh escapes me, and I run my fingers through my hair, frustrated. I've known Grayson long enough to know when something's off. And this? This is off. His phone is on the nightstand, face down. I don't pick it up, but I'm struck by how still the room feels. I can't shake the feeling that something's broken here—something that isn't just the mess. I stand up, pacing the room momentarily, trying to figure out what to do. The silence is unbearable. There's nothing but the quiet hum of the city outside the window. My heart beats too fast in my chest, and the air in the room feels suffocating, like the walls are closing in.

I glance back at Grayson, who's still unconscious, and something tugs at me—a mix of disappointment and worry. This isn't how I expected to find him or how I wanted to see him. I thought there was more to him than... this.

"Come on, Grayson," I whisper to myself, kneeling by his side again. But there's no answer. No movement. Just the faintest rise and fall of his chest.

And I don't know what to do anymore. So I wait.

I sit in the corner, my legs pulled up to my chest as I stare at the floor, waiting, though I don't know what for. Maybe for him to wake up and make sense of all of this. Maybe for him to tell me it's all just a misunderstanding. But the truth is, that's not going to happen. Not here. Not like this. The room feels like it's pressing in on me. It's a different kind of silence now, one thick with the weight of everything I haven't said.

And then, after what feels like an eternity, Grayson stirs. His hand twitches, his breath catches, and his eyes snap open. His gaze immediately lands on me, confusion flashing across his face. His fingers twitch as he tries to sign something, but it's clear he hasn't fully woken up yet; his movements are slow.

"What are you doing here?" he signs, his brow furrowing in disbelief.

I stay quiet, my hands folded in my lap. He doesn't seem to care that I'm here. Not really. Without saying another word, he stands—completely naked. He doesn't look at me, doesn't even flinch. He moves like it's no big deal, like I'm not even here. I'm not sure why it stings, but it does.

I shift uncomfortably, forcing my gaze away as he walks past me to the bathroom, his body a blur of muscle and careless abandon. The water in the shower kicks on, and I let out a long breath, trying to push away the tension that has coiled tight in my chest. He's like a storm, untamed and impossible to control, and I no longer know how to be a part of it.

I call room service, keeping my voice steady and trying to focus on something else. I ask for coffee, pastries, or whatever they can bring. I also request that the maids come through to clean. By the time Grayson emerges from the bathroom, the room is starting to look less like a disaster zone and more like something I can actually stand to be in. The maids have worked their magic. The mirrors are gone. The room, while still disheveled, is no longer an overwhelming mess.

Grayson's frantic eyes scan the room when he steps out, his towel hanging loosely around his hips. He stops when he sees the mirrors are gone, his breath catching in his throat. His eyes flicker around the room like he's expecting someone to be here that isn't. I wait.

"Where are the mirrors?" he signs, his irritation coming through in the sharpness of his fingers. ***"What did you do with them?"***

I don't hesitate. ***"I got rid of them."*** My tone is firm. ***"And no one saw them."***

For a split second, a look of pure relief crosses his face. His shoulders slump, and I can almost feel the weight lift off him.

But I'm not here to let that moment slide by without saying what's been eating at me. I stand up, crossing the room in a few long strides. I meet his gaze with fire in my eyes, no longer able to hold back the disappointment, the frustration, the worry.

"What the hell were you thinking, Grayson?" My hands fly, sharp and fast. *"You risked everything. Everything you've worked for. Not to mention the incredible gift you have in drumming. The reason people even want to be around you. The reason you're on that stage every night."*

He flinches at the words, but it's the truth, and I can't keep it to myself anymore. *"You've got so much to lose, and you've been throwing it all away. For what? For a few moments of numbness? For the next high? This isn't just about you anymore, Grayson. It's about everything you stand for. About what you owe yourself and the people who care about you."*

His eyes narrow and his jaw tightens. He's avoiding my gaze, but I don't back down.

"You're not the only one carrying this weight," I continue, my disappointment stronger now. *"And this isn't what I wanted to see when I came here. This... this isn't the Grayson I know. This is someone else. Someone I don't recognize."*

He raises his hands to sign something, but I cut him off, my fingers moving faster, sharper now. ***"Don't you dare try to brush this off like it's nothing! I can't watch you destroy yourself like this."***

For a moment, we just stand there. His eyes flicker with something—regret, maybe?—but I don't wait for him to respond. I don't need an apology. I need him to understand.

I take a slow, deep breath, and my hands shake slightly as I finish. ***"You need to get it together, Grayson. Before it's too late. Eat some food."***

I walk out of his room, tension wracking my body. I can't watch this.

Chapter 17
Grayson

It's the next evening when I find myself outside Maddie's door. We're all in the same hotel again tonight—one of those nicer ones the label sprang for because of the double-headliner show. Her room's just a few floors above mine. Close, but still far enough to feel out of reach. The weight of the food bag in my hand feels heavy, and the blanket draped across my arm is a comfort I'm hoping she'll take. I'm nervous. Not the kind of nervousness that comes from performing but the kind that twists your insides and scatters your thoughts, leaving you unsure of what comes next.

I had to ask at the front desk—again. Maddie never texts me her room number. But the second they gave it, I didn't hesitate. I knock softly, but I'm unsure if she'll hear me. So, I wait, eyes focused on the floor, tapping my foot lightly against the ground—something to keep myself grounded, to stop myself from overthinking it. When Maddie opens the door, I take in her face, the same one that haunts my dreams. Her eyes are tired but soften just a little when she sees the blanket.

"Hey," I sign, offering her a small, cautious smile.

"What's all this?" Her fingers move in the air, hesitant, like she's unsure if she should ask.

"We could hang out like we used to," I respond, shaking the food bag slightly in front of her. ***"I brought your favorite food and a blanket. We could watch something like old times."***

She crosses her arms, her face unreadable. But I catch the flicker of hesitation in her eyes, that slight tug of longing. She's trying to act like she doesn't care, but I know better.

"It's not a good idea, Grayson." Her signing is slow and deliberate, and I can feel the uncertainty in her movements. I don't blame her. I've been a wreck.

I know I screwed up, I sign, my hands shaking a little as I speak. ***"I know I've been a mess. But I promise you, Maddie, I'm done with all that. The drugs. It's over. I'm going to get clean."*** The promise feels weak, but it's the truth. I can't go back to that place.

Her gaze softens, but she doesn't say anything. I take a small step forward, offering her the food bag and the blanket. ***"Please. Let me show you. Let me make it right."***

Her eyes search mine, obviously looking for any sign of insincerity. I know she's trying to find a crack, something to hold on to so she doesn't have to believe me. But I'm done with the games. I don't need her to be cautious anymore. I need her to see that I can be better. After what feels like an eternity, she sighs, rolling her eyes and giving me a half-smile. *"You're **lucky I still care.**"* She steps aside, allowing me into her hotel room. I follow her in, setting the food bag on the coffee table and spreading the blanket on the bed. But my heart beats a little faster when she sits down next to me—close, but not close enough.

I turn on the TV, something random, just for background. We don't need anything heavy—just quiet company. I can feel her tension next to me; her body is stiff and her mind is still unsure. But I'm not going anywhere this time. I won't mess it up again. She grabs the remote, flipping through channels without really paying attention. I shift a little closer, testing the waters. I rest my hand on the headboard, a tentative touch. She doesn't pull away, so I slowly, cautiously drape my arm around her shoulders, giving her the space to move if she wants to. But she doesn't.

She leans into me just slightly. It's enough. She doesn't fully believe I'm done with the chaos. I don't fully believe it either, but I have to be. I have to for her. I have to for me.

"Thank you for coming," she signs, her eyes meeting mine, and I feel my stomach tighten.

I squeeze her shoulder, tracing slow, comforting circles on her arm. I wish I could say more and explain everything I'm feeling, but the words don't come.

I rest my cheek against her hair, breathing in her familiar scent. I can't hear her breathing, but I can feel her here—the warmth of her body, the slight shift of her weight as she finally lets herself settle into me. It may not all be okay, but this—this right here—is enough.

And I'll take it.

The morning light creeps through the window, soft and warm, and I stir, blinking away the remnants of sleep. For a second, everything is a blur. The sheets are unfamiliar, and I feel a weight on me—someone next to me. I freeze. Confusion rises like a wave, and I'm unsure where I am. I take a moment to collect myself, but the reality sinks in: Maddie's room.

I glance down and there she is, curled against me, her head on my chest, her hair tangled in my fingers. I'm lying on my back, her slight form pressed close to mine. For a moment, I just lay there, feeling the rhythm of her breath against my chest, and something in me loosens. It's peaceful here. It's...right. I could get used to waking up like this; the weight of her presence a comfort I hadn't felt in a long time. But then, as my mind fully wakes, something shifts in my chest—an ache—a pull. I feel it in my bones. The same familiar craving lurks in the background, tugging at me, gnawing at my insides. I blink it away, trying to ignore it, but it's too much. It always is. I shift slightly, pulling my arm out from under her, trying not to disturb her as I slip out of bed. I glance back at Maddie, her face relaxed, unaware of the storm brewing inside me.

I pad across the room, feeling the need grow inside me with every step. I need to get out of here, away from her. I can't risk waking her with the way I'm feeling. I grab a piece of paper and a pen, scribbling a quick note in bold letters: *I'll be back. Stay here.* I leave it on the pillow, careful not to wake her, and head for the door.

As I step out of Maddie's room, the hall feels too broad, too empty. My heart pounds a little harder, and the ache in my chest deepens. I don't know if it's from the lack of her, the craving, or both. I head for my room, moving on autopilot, my thoughts racing, trying to keep my focus. I can't let myself slip again. Once in my room, the moment I close the door behind me, my eyes flick to the corner. I know exactly where I hid the last of the pills. I step toward them. My fingers twitch in anticipation, my mind screaming to just take one. Just one to make it stop. But I stop myself.

No.

The word hits me like a slap, but it's weak. I want to believe it and convince myself I've learned my lesson, but the hunger inside is raw. I stare at the pills for a long moment, my breath shallow, the urge to give in growing with every second. My hand hovers over them. But then, I pull back, my fists clenched, and I berate myself. You're better than this. I tell myself I can do this. I don't need the pills. I promised Maddie. I need to stay calm and get through the day with her. I can't let the craving take me—not now, not with her.

I close my eyes and picture her—calm, steady, looking at me like I'm worth saving.

That's what I'm holding onto.

I head for the door, forcing my body to move purposefully. No more running. Today, I'm taking control.

Chapter 18
Maddie

The sun is warm against my skin as I sip my coffee, the paper cup heating my hands. The park is alive—joggers passing by, kids chasing each other on the grass, an older couple sharing quiet conversation on a nearby bench. It's peaceful. It should make me feel at ease.

But my focus is on Grayson. He sits beside me, staring into his cup like it holds all the answers he doesn't want to say out loud. His knee bounces—a nervous habit I know well.

I watch him for a moment before asking, *"What was it?"*

His body tenses. He doesn't look at me. *"What do you mean?"*

I shift slightly, turning toward him. *"The drugs, Grayson."* My stomach knots around the question. *"I know about the pills. And I'm guessing coke. But what else?"*

His fingers tighten around the cup, his jaw clenching. He exhales through his nose, shaking his head slightly. *"Maddie..."*

I wait. I don't push. But I don't back down either.

His Adam's apple bobs as he swallows. ***"Does it matter?"*** His hands are unsteady as they move.

"Yes."

He finally looks at me, and the shame in his eyes makes my chest ache. ***"I don't want to do this."*** His fingers tremble as he rubs a palm over his face. ***"Not right now. Not today."***

I take a deep breath, steadying myself. ***"I just... I need to know what I was losing you to."***

His hands hesitate before moving again, slower this time. ***"Everything."*** A pause. ***"Anything that would make it stop."***

I press my lips together, nodding slowly. His answer is vague, but I can read between the lines.

Then his fingers move again, more hesitantly this time. ***"Did you tell Delilah?"***

The worry in his expression makes my stomach twist.

"No." I shake my head firmly. ***"I wouldn't do that to you."***

He exhales, shoulders sagging. ***"She'd never forgive me."***

I hesitate. ***"Maybe you should tell her."***

His eyes flash to mine, panic creeping into his expression. ***"Maddie, no."*** His grip tightens around his cup. ***"She wouldn't understand. She'd look at me differently."***

"She loves you."

"That doesn't mean she'd still trust me."

I don't have a response to that. So I stay quiet.

After a long moment, he lets out a slow breath, shaking his head. ***"Please. Can we just... have today? One good day without this hanging over us?"***

I study the dark circles under his eyes and how his fingers shake even as he grips his coffee. He's trying. I can see that. But I also know the weight pressing down on him, the war inside his head.

I sigh, nodding. ***"Okay."***

Relief floods his face, and he leans back against the bench, exhaling shakily.

"But, Grayson?" He turns his head toward me. ***"We can't avoid it forever."***

He nods, but I don't know if he really believes it.

For now, though, I let it go. I take another sip of my coffee, shifting in my seat. Then, almost casually, I ask, ***"Did you see the gossip columns saying that Delilah and Jensen got engaged?"***

Grayson chokes mid-sip, coughing violently as he spits coffee all over the footpath. Several passing pedestrians jump out of the way, shooting him annoyed looks.

"What the fuck?!" he signs, staring at me like I've suddenly grown three heads.

I bite back a grin. ***"Yeah, it was in all the tabloids a few weeks ago, followed by pictures of Alexander throwing her over his shoulder and hauling her out of a Portland bar."***

Grayson's mouth drops open slightly before he shakes his head. ***"Of course."***

I shrug. ***"Apparently that's all worked out now."***

He exhales sharply, rubbing a hand over his face. ***"She's been in love with him since high school. Same with Jensen and Lily. They're all perfect for each other. I don't know why they fight it."***

I smirk. ***"Stubborn. They're just stubborn."***

Grayson rolls his eyes but doesn't argue. Instead, he takes another sip of coffee—this time cautiously. For the first time in a long time, his shoulders seem just a little lighter.

I hesitate before signing, ***"You know we still have another month before the band goes back on tour. Since Delilah is spending all her free time with Alexander and Jensen is in New York, I thought now would be a good time for you to maybe go home and see your mom."***

The moment I sign *mom*, I know I made a mistake. Grayson tenses so hard his shoulders practically touch his ears.

"No."

He doesn't elaborate, but the word carries a finality I can't refute.

I swallow, glancing down at my cup. After a beat, I force some lightness back into my expression. ***"Why don't we go get some food?*** I sign, glancing at him. ***"There's a diner down the street that does good waffles. Any day can be made better with a good waffle."***

Grayson watches me for a long second like he knows what I'm doing. Then, finally, his shoulders drop just a little. He exhales.

"Waffles, huh?"

I nod, offering him a small smile.

"Fine," he signs, shaking his head. ***"But you're paying."***

I roll my eyes. ***"Deal."***

He pushes off the bench, stuffing his hands into his pockets as we start walking down the street. The conversation lingers in the air, unfinished and unresolved.

But for now, I let him have what he asked for.

One good day.

Chapter 19

Grayson

We're walking again.

Neither of us tries to say anything, but it isn't heavy—it's easy. Familiar.

The sun is starting to dip low, casting long shadows across the sidewalk. Maddie's a few steps ahead, her cup cradled between both hands. I watch the wind tug at the curls that slip loose from her clip, the steady rise and fall of her shoulders, calm and unhurried. She gave me space. And it still felt like pressure. She gave me one good day, and all I can think about is how I don't deserve it. A little girl darts past us, laughing, chasing after a dog with zero interest in being caught. I glance at Maddie, then look forward again—

And that's when I see them. A group of kids in the park, playing football. Jerseys too big. Shoes untied. They're shouting—lips wide, arms flailing, tangled limbs and flying grass. It's chaos. And it's familiar. One boy makes a break for it. Dives across an invisible line. Another falls behind him, grinning through the loss. The others erupt around them.

Maddie keeps walking. I don't. I stop. I don't mean to. My feet just freeze. The air goes tight. My pulse kicks up behind my eyes. Dad wanted that for me. Wanted bruises and tackles. Wanted loud games and Friday night lights. Wanted a son who could hear the snap count and crash through a line like he was built for it. Instead, he got me.

I never said it to him—not once—but I always knew. He didn't hate that I was deaf. He hated that I reminded him of everything he wasn't strong enough to handle. I feel Maddie's hand brush my arm. I glance at her.

Her brows are drawn, eyes soft. She signs, **"You okay?"**

I nod. Force it. **"Yeah. Just... memories."**

She doesn't push. Just waits. My fingers twitch like they want to say more. But I don't let them.

Two weeks later, the band meets back up to prep for the final leg. The rehearsal space buzzes with motion—cases wheeled in, mics tested, lights adjusted. I sit behind my kit, sticks in hand, trying to ignore the weight crawling up my spine. Everyone's here. Jensen's talking with the sound engineer. Delilah's arguing about lighting gels. The crew is back in sync as if we never took a break. And I'm terrified I'm going to screw it all up. I don't trust my hands the way I used to. I don't trust myself.

Maddie appears beside me, headset around her neck, clipboard tucked under one arm. She doesn't say anything at first. Just watches me. Then she signs, steady and sure, **"You're *not* alone in this."**

I shake my head slightly, trying to keep my expression even. ***"What if I mess it up?"***

"You won't."

She pauses. Then adds, ***"And even if you do—I'll still be here."***

That one hits me low and hard. I nod once. Not because I believe it completely. Because I want to.

That night, after Maddie falls asleep curled against my chest, my phone buzzes on the nightstand.

I slide it toward me, careful not to wake her.

Knox: *We f*cking did it. Signed. Not Revelation. Better. You coming out or what?*

My stomach flips. I glance down at Maddie. Her breathing is slow and steady. One arm is draped over my stomach. She looks so peaceful and sure.

But I'm not. I gently ease out from under her, holding my breath like I'm afraid she'll feel the shift. She stirs but doesn't wake. I kiss her shoulder, soft and guilty, and slide off the bed. I don't grab my sticks. Don't grab my jacket. Just my phone and my keys. Outside, the night hits me like a jolt—cool air, buzzing neon, pulsing bass somewhere down the block.

I text Knox.

Me: *On my way.*

I don't know what I'm walking into. But I already know it's going to hurt.

The bass hits so hard that it rattles through my bones. It's not music. It's a pulse. A vibration that replaces thought. The club is packed—sweaty bodies grinding under strobe lights, everything too fast, too loud, too much. I can't hear it, but I can *feel* it. I'm on my second beer. Maybe third. I promised myself I'd just take the edge off.

And then Knox is there, wide-eyed and flying high like he never left the scene. He claps a hand over my shoulder, laughing, saying something I don't bother trying to read. His signs are half-assed. Sloppy. He presses something into my palm. Blue. Small. Familiar. I stare at it for a second, which is too long. He shrugs, already moving on. No pressure. Not his problem. My fingers curl around it.

One won't hurt. Just one. I deserve this. I tuck it into my mouth and swallow dry. It's smoother than I remember.

The warmth spreads slowly and steadily. My muscles unwind, and my chest loosens. For the first time in weeks, I stop bracing for impact. The lights get softer around the edges, and the crowd feels less suffocating. I smile. I actually *smile.* Someone offers me another drink. I take it. Not fast—controlled. Measured. Everything feels easy. I tilt my head back and let it sink in. The high. The hum. The *freedom.* And then Maddie flickers in my mind.

The way she signs, **"You're *not alone in this.*"**

The way her brows pinch together when she's trying not to cry.

The way she curled against me in bed like she belonged there.

My stomach tugs just a little. But I shove it down. I'm fine. I'm still standing. I haven't lost control. She'd be mad if she knew. Disappointed. But she's not here. And I'm not out of control. I take another sip and laugh at something Knox signs that doesn't even make sense. I don't care. I laugh anyway. Because for the first time in a long time... I feel good. That should terrify me. But it doesn't.

Not yet. I don't know how long I stay at the club. It could be an hour. It could be three. Time bends around me, soft and slow. Every light smears like wet paint. Every touch is warm. Loose. Easy. I'm not drunk. Not really. I'm not *wasted*. I'm just... high. High and floating. High and *good.* Better than I've felt in weeks.

There's a girl with glitter on her cheeks who leans into me when I walk by. She laughs at something I didn't say and touches my arm. I let her. For a minute, I even think about going back with her.

But the image that fills my head isn't hers.

It's Maddie's.

Maddie with her glasses off, her mouth parted, and her hair wild across the pillow. Maddie, flushed and soft beneath me, nails in my shoulders, lips on my skin. My cock stirs in my jeans, hard and aching.

Shit.

I press a hand to my face and laugh low to myself. Maybe I should've let the glitter girl come. Maybe I'm better off just—*finishing this myself.*

Or maybe... My room's not far. The night air hits me as I step out of the club. Cool. Sharp. Real. I shove my hands in my pockets, head down, breath fogging in the dark. I don't remember walking all the way back. Don't remember swiping my key. Just remember the door closing behind me. The room is dark. Quiet. Still. But not empty. There's a shape in the bed. A soft sigh. A shift beneath the covers.

I smile to myself. Of course.

Some fan? Some warm body I brought back? Doesn't matter. Not really. In my head, it's her. It's always her. And just like that, the fantasy takes over. My Maddie.

Waiting.

Wanting.

I smile as I cross the room. Unsteady. Buzzing. Hard. I don't ask. I don't need to. Because tonight, it's her.

Even if it isn't.

Chapter 20
Maddie

The sound wakes me. Not the TV. Not an alarm. The soft click of the door and the shuffle of feet across the carpet. I sit up fast, heart in my throat.

Grayson. He stands just inside the door, unsteady, shirt untucked, curls damp with sweat. He looks wrecked—exhausted, drunk, but alive. My chest tightens. *Thank God.*

"Grayson?" I whisper to myself, my voice hoarse.

He doesn't sign. Doesn't respond. Just blinks at me, like it takes a few seconds for his brain to catch up. His movements are slow, too smooth. He smells like alcohol. Like a party I wasn't part of. Like a relapse waiting to happen. Anger sparks under my skin, hot and immediate. He left me. He snuck out. And now he's stumbling back in like I don't matter. I push the covers off and slide to the edge of the bed, signing sharp and fast, ***"Where were you?"***

No response. Just glassy eyes and the soft whisper of his feet on the carpet as he steps closer.

"You left me. While I was sleeping. No note. No text. Nothing." Still nothing. He's too far gone. Or maybe he doesn't want to answer. I can't tell.

But then he drops to his knees in front of me. His hands find my thighs like they're the only solid thing in the room. His head bows against my stomach. My breath catches. I don't know if he knows it's me. I don't know if he's here *for me.* But he's here. And I hate that it's enough. His hands slip under my shirt, rough and warm. His mouth brushes skin, slow and reverent.

"Grayson, wait." I grab his wrist, heart racing.

He looks up at me, and for a second, I think he sees me. Really *sees* me. Then he leans forward and kisses my stomach like I'm someone else. Like I'm a memory. A ghost. My chest cracks open.

"It's me," I sign slowly, trembling. *"Maddie. I'm here."* There is no answer. Grayson drops his shirt on the ground and unbuckles his belt. Rough hands pull me close, pushing my pajama bottoms onto the ground. When my top goes over my head, his lips find mine, and he kisses me like he can't bear to stop.

And God help me, I let him. Because I've wanted this for so long. The weight of him. The way he touches me like he's desperate. The heat in his eyes, even if it's glazed over and a little lost. His mouth finds mine again. Hot. Uncoordinated.

Hungry. When he pushes me back against the bed, grinding down, everything else falls away. The betrayal. The fear. The ache I've carried since the first time I realized I loved him.

I should stop this. But I don't. I sign against his chest, fingers brushing skin, ***"Condom. Drawer."*** He fumbles. Finds it. Tears it open with shaking fingers. I help him—because I *need* this too much not to. When he thrusts inside me, it's like something snaps loose in my chest. I arch into him, breathless. It's rough, a punch to my core, and God help me I love every inch.

"Grayson," I sign against his neck. **"You're *here*. I've got you."**

I don't know if he feels it, but I say it anyway. Because even if he doesn't know it's me—even if he forgets by morning—I need this. And for tonight, that's enough. He kisses me like he's drowning and I'm the only thing keeping him above water. Every brush of his lips is rough and searching. His hands roam my body like I am made of precious glass. His mouth finds the curve of my breast, teeth scraping lightly, tongue following. I gasp and arch into him, threading my fingers into his hair.

"More," I sign, chest heaving.

In response, he presses his mouth to my skin, his breath hot and rough—wordless but not quiet. His touch is greedy and reverent all at once, fingers dragging down my ribs, thumbs grazing the sensitive skin. Then he's moving with a low, urgent exhale, spreading my thighs wider, his pace as wild and reckless as he is. I cup his jaw, forcing him to meet my eyes.

"I'm here. I'm real. I want this," I tell him.

His gaze flickers—like he's trying to focus—but all I see is hunger. His eyes darken as he takes me in, every breath from his lips heavier than the last. Our bodies move, and I can feel my wetness coating my thighs. He leans down and kisses my nipple, biting slightly, and I can't help the moan that leaves my mouth. Grayson grins and then kisses higher, his teeth grazing the side of my neck and an earlobe, then higher until our lips meet again. My hips are lifting, meeting his rhythm, and my thoughts are unraveling fast.

"Grayson," I gasp, breath catching. My head falls back. He groans low and shifts up, bracing himself on one forearm as his hand trails down, fingers teasing then swirling in tight circles around my clit. My whole body jolts.

"Please," I sign one-handed, the other clutching the bedsheet.

His mouth crashes into mine again, all tongue and teeth, and I taste the night on him alcohol and desperation and something sharp with need. His cock pumps harder, faster, and I cry out, wrapping my legs around his waist. The tension builds fast, white-hot and blinding. His rhythm falters like he's chasing something inside himself, and I meet him thrust for thrust, giving as much as he takes. Sweat slicks our skin. The room is dark, warm, and quiet except for the sound of breath and skin and the sharp, stuttering gasp I can't bite back.

When I come, I shatter around him, nails digging into his shoulders, lips parted in a soundless scream. He follows with a ragged groan, buried deep, his whole body shaking as he presses into me one last time and finally goes still. We stay tangled like that heaving, silent, ruined. And even though everything in me screams that this will break me come morning, right now, I don't care. Because I got to touch him like this. Feel him like this. Be *his* even if just for tonight.

The room is quiet, the air warm with leftover heat and tangled sheets. Grayson has played my body like the drums he loves all night. I must've dozed off. The sky outside the window shifts from navy to violet, the earliest edge of morning brushing against the skyline. I blink blearily toward it, my chest still aching from everything we just did—from everything I feel.

Then I feel his mouth on me again. Hot. Wet. Intentional. Grayson shifts behind me, one hand curling around my hip, the other anchoring against my lower back as he kisses his way down the curve of my spine. His stubble scrapes lightly over my skin, followed by the soft graze of lips and tongue.

My breath catches.

"Grayson..." I whisper, throat raw.

He can't hear me but his movements slow for a beat, like he felt something shift. Like he sensed it anyway. Then he presses forward, guiding me gently until my knees find the edge of the mattress. Then he shifts behind me, propping himself up and guiding me gently onto my stomach. I follow his lead, breathing unevenly as he slides lower along the bed, lips brushing a line down my spine.

His hands skim over my hips, coaxing me to lift just enough for him to settle between my thighs. His mouth finds me slow and unhurried at first, tongue flicking, curling, dragging until my legs tremble. Until I'm gripping the comforter to stay grounded, the rhythm of his touch unraveling everything inside me.

God... My hands fist in the sheets. I rock back into his mouth, and he growls, fingers digging into my hips to keep me steady. And then he's standing, lining up behind me, the blunt head of his cock teasing through slickness. His breath is hot against my shoulder. He doesn't ask. Doesn't need to.

I arch my back, pushing into him. "Yes. Please. Again."

He thrusts in deep. I cry out high, broken. My head falls forward, forehead pressing to the mattress. Grayson pounds into me relentlessly. The sun begins to rise. Pale gold and pink flood across the floor, casting a soft light over the room and our bodies, and this moment already feels like it exists outside of time.

He moves with purpose now, hips snapping forward in sharp, punishing thrusts. His fingers tangle in my hair, pulling gently until I'm upright again—chest lifted, back arched. He presses in harder. His free hand pinches and twirls my nipple, sending jolts of pleasure through my already overwhelmed system.

I reach one arm back to grab for him. He takes my hand, twining his fingers with mine as he fucks me harder, deeper, each thrust punching little gasps out of my throat. Tears sting my eyes. Not from pain. Not even from pleasure. But from the truth curling around my ribs: *Once the sun fully rises, nothing will be the same.*

Not between us. Not inside me. But even knowing that, I don't stop him. Because I've waited too long for this. I've dreamed of this. And if I only get one night, I'll take every last second. He drives into me again hard and deep and I unravel. My body convulses around him, legs shaking, heart breaking. He follows with a ragged moan, hips stuttering before he spills inside me, his hand still clutching mine like a lifeline. We collapse forward together, breathless. And as the sunrise slips across the bed and paints our skin gold, I know I'll never forget this.

Even if he does.

Chapter 21

Grayson

The first thing I notice is the headache. Not a hangover—just a dull, throbbing pressure behind my eyes. Enough to remind me I'm not clean anymore. My mouth's dry. My body feels like it's been buried in concrete. The bed beside me is empty. Sheets twisted low. Still warm. I sit up slowly, heart pounding, throat dry. My skin is sticky. My thighs ache. And the air still smells like sex—thick and sour. Sweat. Skin. The echo of something I never should've done.

I close my eyes, trying to rewind. Bits come back. A body. Warm. Willing. My hands on her hips. My mouth on her throat. The desperate, breathless rhythm of needing something—someone—so badly I didn't care who it was. But it wasn't her. It couldn't have been.

Maddie wouldn't have let it happen like that—not when I was high. Not when I was gone. I stumble to the bathroom, gripping the sink like it might hold me up. My reflection looks like a stranger. Eyes bloodshot. Skin gray.

What the hell did I do?

I used. I brought someone back here. And I let myself pretend—just long enough to believe it was her. Long enough to feel good. Long enough to ruin everything.

What the fuck is wrong with me? I stare at my reflection. Bloodshot eyes. Pale skin. A red mark on my collarbone I don't remember getting. My jaw aches. My hands shake. I don't remember her face. I don't even care who it was. All I cared about was the fantasy. And now I have to live with the wreckage. Thirty days. Gone. Trust? Shattered. Maddie? Gone too. Because once she knows what I did, she won't stay. She can't.

I glance at the bed. No bra on the floor. No dress in the corner. No evidence. Just the silence. Just me. I grab my phone. There are no texts, no missed calls. Nothing. My stomach flips. Guilt crashing hard and fast. I didn't just fuck up. I lost her.

I feel the vibration in the floor before I see her—the shift of air pressure—and then she's there. Maddie. Hair up, leggings on, and wearing my hoodie, arms full—coffee cups in a tray, a brown paper bag in one hand. She looks... normal. Like this is just another morning. Like I didn't blow everything to hell.

I stagger out of the bathroom, eyes wide, chest heaving. I sign before I can stop myself. ***"I'm sorry."***

She pauses, confused. ***"Maddie, I'm so sorry. I messed up."*** I drop the signs fast and clumsily, panic building. ***"I used. And***

I—God, I didn't mean to—I didn't know what I was doing—"

Her brow furrows. ***"I cheated on you."*** The words burn as I throw them into the air between us. My whole body shakes. ***"I thought it was you. It wasn't you. I brought someone back. I swear to God I didn't mean to. I didn't—"*** My hands fall.

She doesn't say anything. She just stares at me. And I don't know what's worse. That she's silent or that she still hasn't left. We don't talk the rest of the morning. She rides silently to the venue, a coffee cup in one hand, her clipboard in the other. She doesn't look at me once. I think about signing her name halfway through the drive just reaching out, just once.

But I don't.

I keep my hands still, clenched in my lap. Because if I ask her to look at me now, I don't think I'll survive it. She's already moving at the venue before the van stops—issuing instructions, answering questions, directing chaos like nothing happened.

Like I didn't ruin everything last night.

The tension backstage is sharp enough to cut skin. First show back after the break. Big crowd. Bigger expectations. Energy is high, but the mood's off. Delilah's on edge. Jensen's distracted. And Maddie? She's in overdrive... She's running point on lighting cues, arguing with the stage manager, and giving orders to the new intern, who's already two steps behind. But she won't come near me. Every time she passes, her eyes skate right past mine. Like I'm part of the wall. Like I don't exist.

And maybe that's fair. Perhaps I don't.

It's twenty minutes to showtime when I glimpse her by the far dressing room—phone to her ear, her back to the rest of us. She's not talking. Just standing still. Clipboard at her side. Shoulders tight. She hangs up and stares down the hallway for a long moment before turning and walking straight past me, expression unreadable.

She doesn't even flinch when she sees me. And somehow, that's worse than yelling. Worse than silence. Because I'm not even worth reacting to anymore.

Chapter 22
Maddie

When the final pre-checks are done, the energy is thrumming, electric. I find Delilah in her dressing room, just finishing zipping up her last boot.

The chaos is the only thing keeping me upright. If I stop moving or working, I'll feel too much. And I can't afford that. Not tonight. Not when Grayson—I shove the thought away before it can root deeper.

"We are T-minus twenty to the opening act," I inform her, flipping through my clipboard. "We need to get you wired up."

She glances up. "I never did see Dravyn. Did you tell him to come see me?"

"I haven't seen him either," I say automatically, my eyes flickering toward the hallway—half-hoping, half-dreading that Grayson might appear.

He doesn't.

Delilah checks her phone, muttering under her breath. "X still hasn't texted me back either. When I get my hands on that man, he will regret the day he was born."

I clear my throat, suppressing a smile I don't really feel.

She glances up at me, narrowing her eyes. "Oh, don't look at me like that. You know what I mean."

Shaking my head, I follow her out of the dressing room, weaving through the buzzing crew. The closer we get to the stage, the louder the crowd's roar grows, pressing against my chest.

Then, as we step into the wings, Delilah turns to me. "Maddie, are you sure you're okay with being in LA full-time?"

The question catches me off guard, and for a moment, I falter.

"I know you joined us to get experience and travel," she continues, her expression softer now. "I would hate to lose you. You're the best PA, but I don't want you to give up your dream because you're afraid you'll be out of work."

My stomach twists. *What is my dream anymore?* I wrap my arms tighter around myself before forcing a smile. "No, I'm sure it'll be fine. Who knows what the future holds, right? Things can change at the drop of a hat. I do know that I love working with Wild Child Reckless, and these past few years have been the best of my life."

Delilah gives me a soft, knowing look before pulling me into a quick hug. The tech team swarms her, clipping her mic into place the minute she lets go.

I take a step back, the crowd's anticipation vibrating through the air, and then—"Ladies and gentlemen, please welcome Alexander Reckless to the stage!"

I freeze.

The applause is hesitant at first, uncertain. Then Alexander strides out, and the stadium erupts. I turn just in time to see Delilah's jaw drop, her entire body going rigid. Then X steps up to the mic.

"Good evening, Memphis," he says, his voice smooth and confident. "My name is Alexander. You've probably seen me in the papers lately, but there's more to the story than you've read."

My breath catches as he turns, eyes locking on Delilah. He holds out his hand. I watch, transfixed, as she steps forward. The crowd loses their minds, and X starts to speak words that make my chest ache with a bittersweet longing I can't stop. He sings for her. A song that's raw, honest, and filled with love. And when the final note fades, he drops to one knee. The stadium shakes with the force of the cheers, but all I can hear is the thundering of my own heart as I watch Delilah crumble, falling to her knees in front of him. I press a hand over my mouth, my emotions tangled in ways I don't have time to unravel. Because as I watch

Delilah say yes, as I watch X slip a ring onto her finger, as I watch the way he looks at her like she hung the stars...I can't help but wonder: Will anyone ever look at me like that?

No. No, they won't. Not if I stay with someone who's already slipping through my fingers. Not if I let myself believe that dreams like that are meant for people like me.

Dreams are dangerous.

And I don't have room for dangerous anymore.

I don't remember how I got back to the hotel. The whole night blurs together the cheers, the tears, the flashing cameras. I smiled when I was supposed to, nodded, laughed, and kept everything moving like a good PA should.

And now...Now I'm here. Alone. I drop my clipboard onto the desk, press my forehead to the cool glass of the window, and stare out at the Memphis skyline. It's beautiful. It's everything I thought I wanted when I left home. And it's never felt emptier. I close my eyes and for a second, just a blink, just a breath, I see him.

Grayson, standing on a stage bathed in soft light.

No guitar. No drums. No microphone.

Just him.

His hands moving with slow, aching certainty.

"Only you," he signs, the words forming between us like a promise he never made. The image is so vivid it steals the air from my lungs. I hug my arms tightly around myself, fighting the way my heart tries to believe it. Because it's not real. It never was. Not for me. Maybe for Delilah and Alexander. Maybe for people who deserve happy endings. But not for the girl who let herself fall for someone who was never ready to catch her. I breathe shakily, grounding myself in the feel of the glass and the quiet hum of the city beyond.

I push away from the window, grabbing the nearest distraction—emails, schedules, anything to keep my hands busy and my heart locked down tight. Because if I don't... I know exactly who I'll break for. And I can't survive that again. My phone buzzes on the desk, lighting up with a text from Cora. Just a simple question.

Cora: *Still planning to meet after the tour?*

My fingers hover over the screen for a long, long moment. The Maddie from six months ago would have answered without hesitation. The Maddie who still believed things could get better. The Maddie who thought hard work, loyalty, and hope could fix anything. But that Maddie doesn't exist anymore. I pick up the phone, my heart hammering, and press call.

Cora answers on the second ring, her voice warm and easy. "Maddie! Hey—"

"I'm not coming back out after this leg," I say before I can lose my nerve. The words scrape raw on the way out, but I force them out anyway. "I'm sorry, Cora. I—I just can't."

There's a pause. Then, a soft exhale. "You don't have to explain," she says, gentler now. "I get it. I really do."

I press a trembling hand to my forehead, squeezing my eyes shut. "Thank you," I whisper.

"Always," Cora says. "I'm proud of you, Mads."

The call ends.

And for the first time all night, I let the tears fall.

Chapter 23

Grayson

The party's in full swing when I get there. The banner over the bar says *Good Luck, Maddie!* in bold, ugly letters someone clearly slapped together last minute. There's pizza on folding tables, half-drunk bottles of cheap champagne, bad music blasting from a speaker that keeps cutting out.

It's supposed to be a celebration. It feels like a funeral. I stay near the door, beer in hand, trying to look like I belong.

I don't. Not tonight. Not with the way Maddie is shining under the shitty lights—smiling too big, laughing too hard, hugging everyone like it doesn't kill her. Like she's not about to walk out of my life for good. I take a long pull from my beer, hoping it'll dull the sharp edge carving through my chest.

It doesn't.

Law, Mia's bodyguard, gets to her first, pulling her into a bear hug that nearly knocks her drink out of her hand. Jensen's next, tossing an arm around her shoulders and mussing her hair like an annoying little brother. Delilah catches her in a real hug, the kind where you can see them both squeezing too tightly. I watch it happen from across the room—Maddie laughing, crying, trying to hold it together.

And I feel it. The slow, sick twist of loss settling into my bones. She hugs everyone. Except me.

Later, when most of the crowd has thinned out, I find her at the bar, swirling her drink, staring at nothing. The music's softer now. The lights dimmer. It feels like the whole world is holding its breath. I move toward her before I can stop myself. I tap lightly on the bar to get her attention, and she looks up.

"You okay?"

When she smiles, it's brittle at the edges, and her cheeks are flushed from drinking. Her mouth forms the words slowly enough for me to catch. "Time to move on."

Something inside me fractures. I should leave it there. Should walk away. But I can't. Her fingers brush my wrist—barely there, just a ghost of a touch—and it shatters every scrap of self-control I have left. I crash into her—mouth to mouth, hands greedy and clumsy. Maddie gasps into the kiss, and I take it as permission. I grab her hips, yanking her closer, feeling the tremble running through her body and matching my own. The kiss turns frantic, desperate, teeth clashing, breathless. Every part of me is scream-ing that this is wrong, that this is a terrible idea. But her hands are in my hair, her body pressed tight against mine, and I can't hear anything else. I grip the back of her neck, tilting her head so I can deepen the kiss—biting, sucking, devouring.

She moans into my mouth, and I lose it completely. We stumble back to my room, nearly tearing the door off its hinges getting inside. The second it clicks shut, it's chaos.

Maddie's jacket hits the floor. I shove my hands up under her shirt, yanking it over her head, desperate to touch, to taste, to memorize. She yanks my shirt off in return, her nails scraping down my chest in a way that has me growling low in my throat.I slam her back against the wall, lifting her by the thighs. She wraps her legs around me without hesitation, grinding down hard enough that it's almost painful.

Almost.

I duck my head, dragging my mouth down her throat, biting hard enough to leave marks she'll see tomorrow— if she even stays that long. Her hands fist in my hair, tugging me back up to kiss her again, sloppy and frantic. It's not sweet. It's not slow. It's messy. Desperate. Two people tearing each other apart because it's easier than admitting they're breaking. I yank her panties down with one hand, barely getting them off one leg before I'm lining up against her. She pants into my ear, clutching at my shoulders. And when I thrust into her, it's not careful. It's a claiming. A desperate, aching need to feel her one last time. To brand her into my skin so I don't forget. She's tight, wet, perfect around me—so perfect I have to bite down on my lip to keep from losing it too fast. Maddie's nails dig into my back, her head falling back against the wall with a silent cry. I thrust harder, faster, chasing something we both know we can't have.

Every time I move, her breath stutters, every gasp a tiny, beautiful crack in the armor she's tried so hard to build. Her eyes flutter open, locking on mine. And for a second, it's not sex. It's not goodbye. It's just *us*.

Raw. Real.

Everything we are always too scared to say. Her body tightens around me and I know she's close. I shift, angling my hips, and she falls apart in my arms—biting down on my shoulder to muffle her scream. The feel of her clenching, shaking around me drags me over the edge too fast, too hard. I come with a rough gasp against her neck, holding her so tightly I'm afraid I might crush her.

Maybe I want to. Maybe I want to hold her so tight she can't leave. For a long, long moment, we just breathe—clinging to each other like the broken, reckless fools we are. But then reality slams back in. Maddie untangles herself first. Sliding down my body, grabbing her clothes, pulling them on without a word. I move without thinking—lifting my hands, my signing shaky, broken.

"Stay."

She freezes for half a heartbeat. I see it—the way her shoulders tense, the way her whole body fights itself. Then she shakes her head.

Slow. Final.

Her lips move. "I can't." And before I can find a way to change her mind—before I can drag her back into my arms where she belongs—she's gone. The door shuts behind her. And for the first time in a long, long time, I don't just feel lost. I feel hollow.

Chapter 24
Maddie

Two Months Later

The bathroom light is too bright. It hums overhead, sharp and insistent, spotlighting everything I'm trying not to feel. I sit on the bathtub's edge, hands trembling around the plastic stick. The seconds are unbearably long. My heart pounds so loudly that it fills the tiny room.

Not now. Not like this. The test darkens. Two lines.

Positive.

A sharp breath punches out of me. Nausea rises fast and brutal — not the first wave I've had this week. I'd blamed stress. Long hours. Sleepless nights. Anything but this. I press both hands to my face, breathing through the panic. I can't do this. I *have* to do this.

A knock rattles the door. "Mads? You okay?" Lily's voice floats through — low, casual — like the ground isn't caving under me.

I clear my throat. "Yeah! Just a minute!" I shove the test deep into my purse, splash cold water on my face, and force myself upright. There's no time to fall apart. Not today.

Today is Delilah's wedding.

Today is supposed to be about *happily ever afters* — not about unraveling quietly from the inside out. The dressing room hums with last-minute chaos — whispered jokes, clinking champagne glasses, the rustle of silk and lace. Delilah stands at the mirror, radiant and steady, her smile wide and sure.

I cross to her, clipboard clutched tight. "Dee, the guests are ready when you are."

Delilah turns, her face softening as she looks at me. "Thanks, Maddie. Are you okay, babe?" The concern in her voice nearly undoes me.

"I'm fine," I lie smoothly. "Just ready to get home and see my family."

She squeezes my arms but doesn't push.

Across the room, Alexander's mother pulls Delilah into one last tearful hug. James — Delilah's brother — stands ready, offering his arm.

"You ready, brat?" he teases.

"More than ready," Delilah says, laughing.

James grins. "Then let's go get your happily ever after."

The music swells faintly from the other side of the doors. Guests shift in their seats and anticipation crackles in the air. I step back into the shadows, one hand drifting to my stomach.

A secret.

A silent, terrifying truth blooming inside me.

The reception is already in full swing when I make it outside. Twinkling lights weave through the trees, spilling a golden glow over the tables and dance floor. The air smells like barbecue and buttercream. Laughter rises everywhere bright, alive, full. I hover at the edge of it, clutching a glass of lemonade — definitely lemonade — between both hands.

For a second, I just stand there letting the scene wash over me — the voices, the music, the clink of glasses — and memorizing the feeling of being surrounded without belonging.

"Hey," a voice says beside me.

I turn to find a tall guy with sharp eyes and a lazy grin, the kind that says he already knows too much. "You must be Maddie," he says.

"And you're Ransom," I reply, offering my hand.

He shakes it firmly, no-nonsense. "Heard a lot about you," he says, jerking his thumb toward James. "Mostly, you're the only reason this circus didn't burn to the ground."

I laugh — quietly — caught off guard by the compliment. "I think you've been lied to."

"Nah," he says easily. "Ran background. You're impressive."

My eyebrows lift. "You ran a background check on me?"

Ransom just shrugs, unapologetic. "Occupational hazard."

James rolls his eyes in the background. "Ignore him. He's got a God complex."

"God complex and excellent instincts," Ransom quips. "Good call on escaping while you still can."

"Thanks," I say dryly.

He winks and wanders toward the bar, leaving me smiling despite myself and despite the ache clawing up the back of my throat. I tuck myself further into the shadows, letting the celebration swirl around me. So many faces I know. So many memories tied to every laugh, every song, every glass lifted high in the air. And still, I'm already a thousand miles away. Already bracing for the next chapter I'm stepping into alone.

Before I can slip away entirely, Jensen appears at my side, Lily tucked easily into him.

"You hiding out?" Lily teases, bumping my hip with hers.

"Maybe a little," I admit. "It's overwhelming. In the best possible way."

Jensen hands me a napkin folded into some terrible attempt at origami. "Figured you might need a backup flag if you surrender."

I laugh and tuck it into my purse. "I'm not surrendering. Just pacing myself."

"You doing okay?" Lily asks gently, her eyes sharp in that way she has — the way that sees right through me.

"I'm good," I say too fast. "Just excited to get home. It's been a long time since I've seen my parents. My brothers. The ranch."

"Paso Robles, right?" Jensen asks.

I nod, smiling at the sound of home. "Yeah. Feels like a different world compared to all this."

"You deserve some quiet," Lily says warmly. "And a lot of spoiling."

"My dad's already planning a 'surprise' party," I say, rolling my eyes. "He and my brothers can't keep a secret to save their lives."

Jensen chuckles. "You're gonna get mobbed the second you step off the plane."

"I'm looking forward to it," I whisper, blinking fast to clear the burn in my eyes.

"You'll always have a place with us," Jensen says quietly. "Anytime."

The kindness almost breaks me. I nod again, swallowing down the lump in my throat.

Jensen clears his throat, shifting gears. "Speaking of planes — I talked to Jude. He's arranging a private flight for you. Straight to Paso. It's a thank-you from all of us."

I blink at him, caught off guard. "You didn't have to—"

"We wanted to," he says firmly.

Ransom strolls past, catching the tail end. "Plus, Jude loves looking important. Private jets are basically his kink."

I snort into my lemonade, half a laugh, half a sob. "Tell Jude thank you," I say, my voice tight. "Tell all of you thank you."

Jensen smiles, a little tilted, a little bittersweet. "Just promise you'll keep in touch."

"I will," I lie because I want to believe it. But deep down, I know it won't be that simple. Not once the truth comes out. Not once everything changes.

The music shifts again—it's a slow song now. Couples sway under the fairy lights, the air thick with love and hope.

I stand still, soaking it all in.

The laughter.

The life.

The version of myself I'm leaving behind. One hand drifts unconsciously to my stomach.

I'm not going home the same girl who left. And sooner or later, someone's going to realize it.

The sleek and sterile jet waits at the end of the tarmac under the heavy Texas sky. A single flight attendant meets me with a polite smile and takes my bag without comment. The inside of the plane is quiet—leather seats, soft lighting, and polished floors that reflect a version of me I barely recognize. I drop into a seat by the window, buckle in, and press my forehead lightly against the cool glass. The world outside blurs, lights stretching into lines as the engines hum to life.

Goodbye.

Not just to Texas.

To everything.

As the plane lifts off, my stomach drops — a rush of gravity that feels too much like falling. I reach into my purse blindly, fingers brushing against the crumpled napkin Jensen gave me. The terrible little origami flag. I clutch it tightly, squeezing it into my palm as if I can hold onto all the good things. The people I'm leaving behind. The girl I used to be. Tears slip down my cheeks, silent and relentless, before I can stop them.

I press a hand to my stomach, whispering a promise to the tiny life growing there.

I'm going to do better.

I'm going to be better.

The stars blur outside the window, distant and indifferent. And somewhere, thousands of miles away, the boy who broke me has no idea what he left behind.

Chapter 25

Grayson

8 months later....

The green room smells like stale beer and sweat.

The floor's sticky under my boots, littered with torn setlists and crushed cans. Someone knocked over a table earlier, and a splatter of red Solo cups is still bleeding across the concrete. No one bothered to clean it up.

Maddie wouldn't have put up with it.

She would've had this place cleaned within five minutes. Maddie wouldn't have let Wild Child Reckless play a low-level gig like this. I sink into a battered chair by the wall, my drumsticks tapping a restless, stuttering rhythm against my thigh. The ache in my wrists hums under my skin — old, familiar — a pulse deeper than blood.

Knox slumps on the couch across the room, his guitar propped against a broken amp, head thrown back like he doesn't have a care in the world.

He pops a pill under his tongue and winks at me.

I don't react. Already took mine. Already counting the seconds until the world softens. A sharp wave from the tech at the door catches my eye.

Showtime.

I push to my feet. My shoulders grind. My muscles scream in protest with every step. Still, I move. Because it's the only thing I know how to do.

The first vibration rolls through the stage under my boots. The crowd is a wall of heat and motion — bodies crashing together, fists pumping the air.

I don't hear them. I **feel** them.

Every stomp, every shout, every bass pulse hammering up through the soles of my feet, rattling my ribs. The house lights blind me in violent bursts as I drop behind the kit. Knox flashes me a savage grin across the stage — wild, wired, electric.

I lift my sticks. Three taps. Downbeat. The set blurs.

Muscle memory moves my arms. The beat is a living thing stitched into my skin — a creature made of bone, breath, and pressure. Snare hit. Tom roll. Cymbal crash.

Every note reverberates through me, crashing like a wave I can't outrun. The floor trembles with the weight of the crowd. The riser shudders beneath me. Pain threads through my shoulders, knees, and wrists. My muscles burn with every snap of my wrists. The vibrations rattle my teeth.

But I don't stop. I can't. Stopping would mean feeling. And I can't afford that. We cut the set short by two songs.

No one notices.

Or if they do, they don't care. The second we hit the last beat, I drop my sticks and shove off the riser, sweat burning down my spine. The hallway backstage stinks — smoke, beer, something sour lurking underneath. I strip off my soaked shirt and let it fall somewhere behind me as I shoulder into the dressing room. It's worse in here — walls pressing in, heavy with stale breath and the sticky aftertaste of another night we'll all pretend was worth it.

The couch sags under Knox's weight, legs thrown wide, a fresh bottle dangling from his fingers. He kicks the table in front of the sofa with his boot when he sees me, lifting the bottle like a lazy toast.

I shrug and drop into the opposite chair, the cracked vinyl shifting under me.

The room vibrates faintly—bass from the stage bleeding through the floor, movement just beyond the walls—but none of it touches the silence inside my head.

I dig through my jacket, fingers closing around the little metal tin. It rattles — two pills left. I tip them into my palm and hesitate long enough to hate myself. Then I swallow them dry.

The numbness creeps up from my gut, winding around my ribs and seeping into my skull. It doesn't make me feel better. It just makes everything... quieter.

Slower.

Safer.

I tip my head back against the wall and close my eyes.

A flash slices through the darkness —blue eyes framed by messy curls, soft hands tugging at my wrist, laughter sparking against the shadow.

Maddie.

The ache is instant.

Brutal.

Tearing through the flimsy shield I put up with pills and booze.

I see her —feel her — so vividly it knocks the breath from my chest.

Her hand catching mine backstage. Her smile was pure and blinding, lighting up places I didn't even know were broken inside me. The way she used to look at me —like I was worth saving. I curl my fingers into fists, nails biting into my palms.

No.

I slam the door shut on it. Hard. Final.

Because she's gone. Because even if she wasn't...even if she stood in front of me right now, offering her hand —I wouldn't know how to reach back. I'm too far under. Too broken. Too late.

The couch jolts as Knox shifts suddenly, throwing himself sideways like a drunk king claiming his throne, waving the empty bottle overhead like he just won something. I catch the motion out of the corner of my eye but don't bother looking directly at him.

Tomorrow, there'll be another city.

Another show.

Another faceless crowd to pretend for.

I'll get up.

I'll play.

I'll smile.

And I'll keep pretending that I'm not already dead inside.

Because pretending is easier than drowning.

And because the only thing worse than pretending...is remembering what it felt like to be alive.

Chapter 26
Maddie

Nine Months After the Wedding

The world narrows to a blur — bright lights, shouted encouragement, the burning ache of one more push.

And then — weight. Warm and new and impossibly small.

"Here she is," the nurse says, and Clara is on my chest a heartbeat later.

She's slippery and squalling, fists flailing in the bright light, her skin flushed red and raw. She kicks out instinctively, tiny legs stronger than they should be, furious at being yanked from the only world she's ever known. I stare at her, stunned at her feel, heat, and heaviness.

And then I see it. The softest dusting of pale blonde hair across her head, already curling against her damp scalp. So light it's almost silver under the fluorescent lights. Grayson's hair. The breath leaves my body in a rush; a cracked, broken sound no one else seems to notice.

She's him. And she's me. And she's everything.

"Clara," I whisper, brushing trembling fingers over her crown. "Hi, baby girl. It's you. It's really you."

The next few hours blur into a fog of hands and voices. Clara is taken for cleaning and weighing. I'm stitched and wiped down, machines beeping softly around me. It's mechanical. Necessary. Nothing feels real until they wheel me into a new room — a bland, beige rectangle with a cheap print of sunflowers on the wall and an empty bassinet by the bed. I sink back against the too-thin mattress, every muscle in my body screaming, every nerve raw. The silence feels wrong somehow — hollow and too big — until they bring Clara back and lay her against my chest again.

I breathe her in. Warmth. Milk. Newness. She's so tiny. A little burrito of pink blankets and soft blonde curls, tucked against my heart like she's always belonged there.

Then there's a knock at the door, soft and hesitant.

Before I can answer, my mom slips inside. She stops short at the sight of us — me pale and battered, Clara nestled against my chest — and presses a hand over her mouth. Tears spill down her cheeks unchecked.

"Oh, sweetheart," she breathes. "She's perfect. Look at her. Another beautiful girl for our family." Her hands shake as she strokes Clara's head, marveling at the fine blonde fuzz and the stubborn set of her jaw.

"You did so good, baby."

I manage a shaky smile.

Behind her, my dad steps into the room. He's usually all noise — heavy boots, booming voice — but now he moves like he's afraid he'll break the air around us. He crosses to my side, leans down, and presses a kiss to my forehead, rough and tender.

"You brought her home safe," he says, voice cracking. "You brought her home."

I close my eyes against the burn behind them, nodding once. The door swings wider, and suddenly, my brothers pile in.

Wyatt — steady and serious.

Luke — grinning, his eyes suspiciously shiny.

Colt — pretending he's too grown to cry but failing miserably.

They hover at the foot of the bed, jostling each other for a better look. Wyatt steps forward first, gently brushing the back of his hand over Clara's cheek.

"You don't gotta worry about a damn thing, Mads," he says, low and firm. "She's got us. Always."

Luke leans over next, tapping Clara's tiny fist with one thick finger.

"She's already tougher than the rest of us put together," he says with a crooked grin.

Colt crouches beside the bed, one hand flat against the mattress like he's grounding himself.

"I'll stake my life on it," he says, voice breaking. "Whatever she needs, whenever she needs it. I swear it."

The weight of it — the love, the promises, the fierce protectiveness — crushes my chest until I can barely breathe.

Later, after they're gone —after my mom promises she'll be back at dawn with real food and Wyatt nearly gets into a fistfight with a nurse about visiting hours —the room falls quiet again.

It's just me and Clara.

I watch her sleep, one hand curled tight against her cheek, the other fisting the air like she's ready to take on the world.

Tears prick at my eyes. Not because I'm sad. Not because I'm scared. Just because it's so much. Love. Fear. Gratitude. Grief.

I bury my face against the top of her soft blonde curls and let the tears come, silent and unstoppable.

"I've got you," I whisper into her hair. "No matter what."

The next morning, the nurse wheels Clara back in after her newborn screenings.

She smiles — kind, careful — and hands her to me with practiced gentleness.

"We did Clara's hearing screen," she says, smoothing down a corner of the blanket. "She didn't pass."

The words settle into the room like dust.

Not loud.

Not sharp.

Just heavy.

"We'll do a retest before you leave," the nurse continues quickly. "Sometimes it's fluid in the ears. But... she may be deaf."

I nod, running my palm gently over Clara's back. "Her father is deaf. So is his mother." It doesn't feel like a tragedy. It feels like a truth — one more piece of who she is. Strong. Stubborn. Brilliant.

Perfect.

The nurse leaves us alone again, and I pull Clara tighter against my chest.

I think about all the things I don't know. The things I'll have to learn. The things we'll have to figure out together. But none of it, none of it scares me more than the idea of not trying.

I kiss her forehead, breathing in her soft baby smell, and whisper the same promise I've already etched into my bones.

"I've got you, Clara. Always."

No matter who left.

No matter who stayed.

No matter how loud or quiet the world is.

She'll never wonder if she's enough.

Not as long as I'm breathing.

Chapter 27

Grayson

6 months later

The first thing I notice is the blood on my knuckles.

The second is the pounding in my skull — a low, nauseating throb that doesn't fade even when I shove upright. The mattress sags unevenly under me, the room spinning slowly and ugly.

The hotel reeks of stale beer, cigarettes, and sweat. One boot's tossed near the door, the other half-kicked under the bed. My jeans are twisted around my waist like I couldn't bother getting them off properly. There's a girl sprawled across the bed's far side—maybe blonde. Or brunette.

Hard to tell in the sick yellow light. I don't remember her name.

Don't want to.

My ribs creak when I stand, and the room lurches sideways. I catch myself against the wall, stomach churning.

One boot's near the door. The other's halfway under the bed. I grab them both, one at a time, fingers clumsy. Tug them on, doing my best to stay quiet .

Then I cross the room, the soles thudding dully against the sticky carpet. The cracked screen of my phone flashes weakly on the nightstand, buzzing once, then dying again. I drag it free, thumb scraping over the spiderweb of broken glass.

Missed messages.

Delilah: *Hey. Haven't heard from you. You good?*

Jensen: *Still family. Doesn't change.*

Mia: *Miss your stupid face, Bongo Boy. Text me or I'm coming after you.*

My thumb hovers over the last one.

Short. Simple.

Mom: *Hope you're safe. Love you. Always.*

The words slice something raw under my ribs.

For a second — half a breath — I think about answering. Just a quick text. Just a lie that says I'm fine. Instead, I kill the screen and shove the phone face-down into the mattress. Can't afford to reach back. Can't afford to feel.

When I climb aboard later, the bus stinks of weed and old fast food, and my hood is yanked low over my head. Knox thuds his boot against the lounge floor — three sharp beats — trying to catch my attention.

I feel the vibration through my boots but don't turn around, and I don't acknowledge him. I drop into the nearest empty seat, every joint stiff and aching. The tin in my jacket rattles when I shift.

I pull it free, dry swallow two pills without thinking — then add another for good measure. The bitter taste burns down my throat.

The high used to hit fast. Now it barely scratches the surface.

We pull up to a bar and stumble inside. It is nothing but a blur of light and movement.

Heat rolls off the bodies packed wall to wall, the bass hammering up through the floor and into my bones.

The vibration rattles the beer bottles on the bar and shakes inside my chest until I can barely breathe. Knox shoves a shot into my hand, grinning wide and wild, his lips moving too fast for me to read.

Doesn't matter. I throw it back without tasting it.

One shot. Another. Another. Swallow. Forget. Repeat.

A fight breaks out near the bathrooms.

I catch it out of the corner of my eye — two guys shoving, fists flying, a table crashing sideways. The vibration spikes under my boots, and the floor trembles like it might split open.

Someone slams into me, spilling beer down my shirt. Without thinking, I swing. Knuckles connect with jawbone — sharp, brutal.

Pain blooms up my arm, bright and clean. For half a heartbeat, the world tilts into slow motion —the crunch of bone, the jolt of impact, the ripple of heat flashing up my wrist. It almost feels good. Almost.

Back on the bus, I slump against the window, my knuckles throbbing, the glass cool against my forehead. The road blurs past in streaks of black and orange. The tin feels almost empty now when I shake it.

I tip two pills into my palm. Hesitate.

Then swallow three instead. No water. No hesitation.

The high doesn't come. Only the slow numbness, the familiar drag in my veins, the way the world dulls around the edges without ever really letting go. I crawl into my bunk, the mattress lurching with every turn of the wheels, and bury my face in the pillow.

The dark presses in around me. Then — a flash.

Blue eyes, stubborn and steady behind thick glasses.

Fingers signing something fierce in the dark.

"Stay," she said once, hands shaking.

Maddie. The memory knifes straight through the haze — clean, brutal, merciless. I shove it down hard, harder than I should, until my whole body aches. She's gone. She's been gone.

I made sure of that.

Tomorrow, there'll be another city. Another bar. Another fight waiting to happen. Maybe tomorrow, I'll hit hard enough that I won't have to get back up. Maybe no one will even notice. Maybe that's the point.

Chapter 28
Maddie

Clara- 1 year old

Clara toddles across the living room floor, fists clenched for balance, her soft blonde curls bouncing with each determined step.

She signs as she goes, clumsy, overexaggerated movements ***"Mom. Up."***

I grin and sign back. ***"Good job."***

Her face lights up, her whole body vibrating with pride. She doesn't need words. We have our own language, and it's enough.

The morning sun pours through the windows, casting warm patches across the worn hardwood floors. Outside, the ranch hums to life Wyatt hammering fence boards, Colt arguing with Luke over who lost the better horse, and Mom bustling in the kitchen. Today, the whole place feels like it's holding its breath, bracing for something bigger, because today isn't just any day.

Today is Clara's first birthday.

I adjust the paper crown sliding sideways on her head, pink, crinkled from her chewing on it earlier, and kiss her hair.

"You're the bravest girl I know," I whisper.

Clara signs something that looks vaguely like ***"More,"*** and giggles, spinning herself into a dizzy stumble. I catch her easily, scooping her up and breathing in her baby-sweet scent milk, sunshine, and stubbornness. There were nights when I first brought her home and sat on the nursery floor, back against the wall, counting her fingers and toes under the moon's pale glow.

Ten tiny fingers. Ten tiny toes.

I counted them over and over, heart hammering in my chest, sure that if I looked away even for a second, something would go wrong. I was searching for proof she was whole. Proof I hadn't already failed her. Some nights, I cried so softly, Clara didn't even stir, tears slipping down my cheeks as I whispered promises into the dark.

I'll do better.

I'll be enough.

I'll protect you from everything, even myself.

Now, watching her stomp her way toward the kitchen, hands flying in excited, made-up signs, I know the truth. She's not the thing that broke me. She's the thing that saved me.

My sunshine. My Clara.

By noon, the house is packed. Neighbors. Family friends. Ranch hands Wyatt insisted we invite. And standing quietly near the gate, Grayson's parents. Grayson's mom spots Clara first, her face breaking into a fragile, aching smile. Before I can say anything, she scoops Clara into her arms, spinning her gently.

Clara signs *"Hi!"* broad, clumsy, perfect and Grayson's mom lets out a choked laugh.

She signs back, slow and sure, *"Hi, beautiful."*

I catch Grayson's dad hovering near the porch, his hands shoved deep in his pockets, his body stiff like he doesn't know how to fit here anymore. But his eyes track Clara's every move, as if she's the only real thing in the world. Clara teeters toward him, goat toy clutched in one hand, crown slipping again. For a moment, it looks like she'll fall. Grayson's dad drops into a crouch stiff, slow, like it hurts him to move.

He braces himself against the porch rail, arms wide but hesitant, giving her the choice. Clara lets out a soft, giddy sound more breath than voice and throws herself into his chest. His hands close around her awkwardly at first, then, more surely, he cups the back of her head and tucks her close, like she's the most fragile, most important thing he's ever held. His face crumples just for a second. He presses his forehead into Clara's soft hair and squeezes his eyes shut. I turn away, blinking hard, throat burning. Because in that one raw, broken moment, it's not just Clara he's holding. It's every piece of the son he lost the son who doesn't even know what he's missing.

The party roars on around us.

Wyatt and Colt are staging impromptu goat races. Luke somehow ends up in the pond with half the cake on his shirt. Mom sets out enough food to feed a small army. Clara claps when the candle is lit, bouncing in my arms, her eyes wide with wonder. Everyone signs the birthday song as we sing clumsy, loud, and perfect and Clara laughs so hard she falls sideways into her goat toy.

The gifts pile up like a mountain.

First, Wyatt and Colt wheel out their handmade goat wagon hilariously lopsided, painted fire engine red. Clara squeals, a breathy, delighted sound, and throws both arms around it, patting the rough wood with her tiny hands. Then Luke presents a battered pony saddle that's way too big and worn smooth from years of use. Clara crawls across the floor, running her palms over the worn leather, tracing the cracks and buckles with fascinated fingers. When Mom hands her a tiny pink dress, Clara crinkles the fabric between her fingers, giggling at the texture. Then, promptly, she shoves the sleeve into her mouth for good measure. And then Grayson's mom presses a small velvet box into my hand.

"I had this made," she signs, her fingers trembling.

Inside is a silver bracelet, delicate and shining, a tiny drum charm dangling from the chain and catching the light.

For a long second, I just stare at it. The charm rocks gently on its chain, catching the sunlight and throwing it back in tiny flashes. A drum. Grayson's drum. Grayson's rhythm. The heartbeat that once carried the band carried me, even when I didn't realize it. My throat tightens so hard it aches. I trace the charm lightly with my thumb before looking up, my eyes swimming.

"Thank you," I sign back, my hands shaking.

Grayson's mom signs slowly, fiercely, *"She's a Stone. Always."* I nod once, no words, no air left to give her. Only gratitude. Only grief.

Later, after the noise dies down and Clara sleeps curled against her goat, I sit alone on the porch swing. The bracelet is warm against my palm.

I close my eyes and tilt my face toward the stars. I wonder, not for the first time, what Clara's future will look like. If she'll ask about him someday the man whose blood she carries, whose laugh she never heard. I wonder if Grayson will ever know the little girl who toddled her way into the world without him and lit it up anyway. If he'll ever deserve her. If he'll ever even try. I tighten my grip on the bracelet, feeling the sharp edge of the drum charm dig into my skin.

"I've got her," I whisper into the dark. "I promise."

Because Clara isn't missing anything. She isn't broken. She isn't less. She's whole. She's mine. And she's the brightest damn thing in my entire world.

Chapter 29
Grayson

The stage under my boots vibrates with the soundcheck. I can feel the rumble in my teeth, the way the bass rattles the floorboards and climbs into my bones. It should be familiar. Comforting.

It isn't.

I shove the venue's back door open, blinking hard against the flashing lights. The hallway is a blur of bodies moving, stagehands shouting silently across the noise. I can't focus. I can barely stand. Pills hum in my bloodstream, heavy and syrupy. Everything feels a half-second too slow.

I shove through the curtain, dragging my kit bag behind me, only to freeze. The drum kit is already set. And it's not mine. There's someone else sitting behind it, head bent low, sticks twirling between nimble fingers.

My place. My stool. My band.

Knox stands near the mic, tuning his guitar and not glancing my way. I step forward, heart hammering not from panic, but from rage. Knox finally looks up. No guilt. No apology.

He signs once, sharp, and final. ***"You're done."***

It takes a second for the meaning to land. And when it does, it detonates in my chest. I charge him before I can think. Before the numbness can swallow it. Knox braces, not even surprised, grabs my jacket by the front and shoves me backward so hard I stumble into the bass amp.

The techs move fast, security faster. Hands close around my arms, my ribs. Yanking me off my feet. Dragging me toward the exit. I thrash once, but it's useless. Dead weight in their grip, they haul me through the side door and into the alley. Concrete scrapes my palms as I hit the ground hard enough to see stars. The door slams shut behind me. The vibrations of the music die out, leaving only the low, dull thud of the city beyond the alley walls.

And me.

Left outside like garbage. I push up slowly, blood in my mouth from where I must have bitten my lip. The streetlights blur, sharp and silver and ugly. I don't know how long I sit there.

Minutes maybe.

Hours.

Long enough for the world to stop spinning. Long enough to feel the crack finally split wide inside my chest. Shoes are moving toward me on the pavement. Expensive shoes. I look up through bleary eyes. A man stands over me crisp suit, polished shoes, disgust curling his mouth like he smells something rotten.

He signs perfectly, ***"Looks like I got here just in time. Impeccable timing, as always."***

I squint at him, confused.

He speaks aloud too, his words careful and professional. ***"Let me introduce myself. Jude Snyder. I work for a man named Jensen Parker. Maybe you've heard of him."***

His hands move easily between signs and words, fluid and sharp. I push up onto my elbows, sneering. I sign back, sloppily, ***"Fuck off."***

Jude smiles and not kindly. Amused. Like I'm a particularly filthy stray dog he's been forced to rescue. ***"And leave you here in this alley to rot?"*** he says lightly. ***"Tempting. Very tempting. But unfortunately, I have a job to do."***

He crouches, careful not to let his tailored pants touch the ground. ***"You have two choices,"*** he signs crisply. ***"Come with me....get a hot shower, some food, maybe even two show-ers..."*** He wrinkles his nose dramatically. ***"...because frankly, I think the puddle you're lying in is piss."***

I glare up at him, rage buzzing under my skin. The urge to swing, to fight, rises thick and hot. He watches it all calmly. Unimpressed.

"Or," he continues, smooth and detached, ***"you can stay here and wait for the cops to pick you up for trespassing, loitering, and public intoxication."*** He shrugs. ***"Your call."***

The cold from the ground seeps into my bones. My hands tremble when I push upright. The pills in my pocket are gone. The band is gone. Even Knox. Gone.

Jude rises smoothly to his feet and holds out a hand. Not offering sympathy. Offering a leash. I stare at it for a long second, hating him. Hating myself more. My fingers close around his wrist hard, bruising. He doesn't even flinch. The car he leads me to is black, sleek, and too clean for someone like me to sit inside. He shoves me in without ceremony, like loading trash into a bin. The city lights smear past the windows in long, liquid streaks. I slump low in the seat, the leather sticking to my skin. Jude drives one-handed, calm as a corpse.

Every so often, he glances over, evaluating and judging. I can feel it radiating off him in waves. ***"You have choices,"*** he signs eventually. ***"Voluntary rehab clean sheets, decent food, therapy with people who don't smell like piss."*** He pauses. ***"Or involuntary."*** He doesn't explain. He doesn't have to.

I stare out the window, my heart pounding too hard to catch my breath. Everything inside me wants to fight. Wants to run. I want to claw my way back to the numbness. But there's nothing left. No one left. No place left to fall. I know when Jude pulls into the circular drive of a pristine white building surrounded by high walls and clipped hedges. This is it. End of the line. Or maybe, maybe, the first fucking step out of the pit I've dug myself into. But it sure as hell doesn't feel like salvation. It feels like surrender.

He kills the engine and turns to me, signing one last time. ***"Choice is yours. Walk in, or crawl in after they drag you."***

I shove the door open and stumble out into the cold, leaving the stink of piss and blood and bad decisions behind. Jude follows not helping, not hurrying. Just watching. Waiting. The lobby looks more like a hotel than a hospital. It has marble floors, fresh-cut flowers, and a soft citrus scent that tries too hard to feel expensive rather than clinical.

Jude signs me in with a clipped nod to the receptionist, all polished confidence and quiet money, and we're immediately led down a private hallway into a small, glass-walled office that overlooks a koi pond. There's no fake plant in the corner just real ones. Trimmed. Alive.

The administrator offers Jude a tablet and a packet of papers for me. Her signs are slow and professional. ***"Thank you for your patience. We were making sure everything was ready for your arrival. Please review and sign these documents. If you have any questions, let me know."***

Jude signs back. ***"I'll handle billing and consents. He's the patient. Just the basic forms for him, please."***

I drop into the chair beside him. The leather squeaks under my weight. I don't look at the papers. Jude taps once.

"Do it."

My name is already printed on the forms. There is just a line waiting for a signature. I grip the pen and sign without looking. If I stare at it too long, I might lose my nerve.

Jude initials his pages silently. No one asks me if I'm ready. No one lies and says this is going to be easy.

A staff member in scrubs tailored, not shapeless meets us outside the admin office. He signs, ***"Mr. Stone? Right this way."*** We move through a quiet corridor lined with wood paneling and soft lighting. They don't ask for my things in the open. Instead, we're shown into a private intake room with frosted glass and a small cabinet in the corner. The staffer opens a drawer, takes out a clear bag, and signs, ***"Please place your belongings here: phone, wallet, jacket."***

I hesitate.

Jude doesn't look at me, but he signs, **_"You knew this was coming."_**

I drop my phone in, then my wallet, then my jacket. The weight of it leaves my shoulders all at once, and I hate how light I feel. The staffer pats down each item carefully and respectfully. When he finds the tin in my inner pocket, he doesn't flinch.

He signs, **_"This will be destroyed. No legal action. We only document."_**

I nod once. He locks the drawer and hands me a new set of clothing soft gray joggers, a white T-shirt, and a hoodie. Everything is neatly folded and very clean.

"Please shower. Then we'll move you to the medical wing."

The bathroom looks like it belongs in a spa ad rainfall shower, dimmable lights, stone tile. But no mirror. The shampoo smells like lavender. The towel is plush. None of it makes a difference. I scrub harder than I should. I try not to think. Try not to feel anything. The clothes fit very well. Nothing itchy. Nothing oversized. Too comfortable for what this place is about to take from me.

Afterward, I'm led upstairs to the medical wing not a hospital room, but close. Crisp linens. Monitors hidden behind discreet cabinetry. A nurse who signs **"We'll _check on you every two hours."_**

I nod. She leaves a glass of water and a set of pills. I don't ask what they are. I lie down. The sheets smell like lavender too. I fucking hate it.

Chapter 30
Maddie

Clara- 2 years old

The morning sun paints the hills in pale gold, warm and lazy against the cool spring air. Clara squirms on my hip, fists signing ***"Go!"*** with impatient little jabs.

"We're going," I promise, grabbing the grocery list and nudging the screen door open with my boot.

We have a party to pull off. A two-year-old's birthday party waits for no one, least of all a single mom running behind. Outside, the ranch hums to life. Wyatt's voice booms from the barn, arguing with Colt about fence repairs. Luke barrels past us, teasing Clara by pretending to steal her goat toy, sending her into giggles.

We make it halfway into town before the truck shudders and pulls hard to the right.

Flat tire.

Of course.

I grip the wheel, muttering curses under my breath as I ease onto the gravel shoulder outside the feed store. Clara kicks her legs excitedly, signing, ***"Stop?"*** With wide, confused eyes.

"Yeah, kiddo. Stop," I respond, rubbing my temples. I swing down, survey the damage, and pop the tailgate to grab the jack.

The sun beats down. The tire iron slips in my sweaty hands. Clara signs, ***"Go? Go?"*** from the passenger seat, her face crumpling when I shake my head.

"Need a hand?" The voice comes from behind me easy, polite.

I turn and find a man leaning against the tailgate next to me, arms folded casually across his chest. Tall. Sun-browned. Baseball cap pulled low over dark hair. Steady eyes.

Teddy Abbott.

I recognize him now as the new vet everyone's been buzzing about. "I'm good," I grunt, jamming the iron harder.

He raises his hands in mock surrender. "I meant no offense. You look like you could beat me in arm wrestling. Just figured I'd offer."

I huff a laugh despite myself. "I'm just late. That's all."

He glances at the overloaded truck bed, which is filled with balloons, cake boxes, and paper plates that threaten to topple. "Big day?"

"My daughter's birthday," I say, tugging stubbornly at the tire.

"How old?"

"Two."

His mouth tilts into a real smile. "Best age. They still think you're magic."

I freeze for a second, caught off guard. He squats beside me without waiting for permission, pries the jack from my hands, and works it loose with a practiced snap.

"Go sit with your kid," he says. "I'll have you back on the road in five minutes." And he does. Silent. Efficient. Not trying to impress anyone.

When he finishes, he wipes his hands on his jeans and tips his head toward Clara, who's pressed against the truck window, frantically waving her goat toy. "You've got your hands full," he says.

"Always," I say with a tired laugh.

"You have just the one?"

"Just Clara."

He smiles again, softer this time. "I love kids. Grew up with a herd of cousins. Kids and goats not much difference some days."

I snort, climbing into the cab. ***Thanks,*** "I say, signing it too, without thinking.

He catches the sign, brows raising slightly, but he doesn't comment. "Anytime," he says instead. "Happy birthday to your little one."

I pull away, tires crunching gravel, feeling a strange lightness settle into my chest. Not flirting. Not rescuing.

Just... helping.

By the time we roll back onto the ranch, Clara's drooping with exhaustion, her head bobbing where it rests against her car seat, goat toy clutched tight in her lap. It's already late afternoon. The sun's dipping low, casting long shadows across the gravel drive. The party starts soon, and I still need to frost the cake, set out chairs, and figure out where the hell Luke left the giant goat cutout.

I swing around back and catch the boys hammering away at something suspiciously rickety behind the barn. I don't ask. I don't want to know. Groceries in hand, I ease the cake box onto the kitchen counter like it's made of glass.

And that's when I hear it.

A thin, high-pitched mewling the kind that hits straight in the chest. I turn toward the sound and see Clara crouched in the yard, goat toy abandoned in the dirt beside her. One small hand is outstretched toward a wobbling puff of fur.

A kitten.

If you can call it that. It's scrawny, shaking, more burrs than body. Patchy fur clings to too-prominent ribs. Its tail drags. One eye's swollen shut. It mews again, sharper this time, but not stronger.

I groan inwardly. "Of course."

Clara turns toward me, signing **"Help?"** with both fists.

I sigh, already moving. ***"You're killing me, kid."***

She watches with wide, serious eyes as I grab a ratty towel from the laundry room and crouch beside the kitten. It doesn't flinch when I scoop it up. That's how I know how bad it really is. The fur is sticky and the skin is too hot. It smells like damp hay and hopelessness.

Clara brushes a hand gently over its matted head, signing, **"Soft. Mine?"**

I don't answer, not right away. I'm already doing the mental math: the vet bill, the chaos, the timing.

"Mads?" Mom's voice floats from the porch. "You almost done out there?"

"Just rescuing something," I call back.

She steps closer and raises an eyebrow when she sees the towel. "Oh, Lord. That girl's heart's going to take over the county."

Clara looks up and signs, ***"Nana! Baby! Hurt!"***

Mom leans down, peeking into the bundle. "She's a mess," she says, but her voice is gentle. "You want me to prep the old crate in the mudroom?"

"Yeah," I murmur, glancing between the kitten and the tiny girl reaching for it like it's already hers. "Thanks."

Clara signs, *"Friend,"* and wraps both arms around her goat, glancing between us like she's ensuring we all understand what matters here.

And we do.

"Come on, sunshine," I sign. *"Let's help your friend feel better before the party."*

She signs, *"Better!"* and she's beaming.

I hoist her onto my hip, kitten and towel tucked carefully in my other arm, and head for the house. Because there's always time for kindness. Even when you're on a deadline.

The vet clinic is cooler inside, a welcome contrast from the dry heat and small-town chaos outside. It smells like cedar shavings and antiseptic, the low hum of the A/C the only real noise. It is peaceful and controlled, like someone tried to package calm and sell it by the hour.

I sign us in at the front counter, and the receptionist waves us to a private room without asking questions. This is what it's like in small towns; everyone already knows who you are and what you're here for. Clara bounces slightly on my hip, clutching the towel like it's holding her whole world. The kitten's head barely peeks out; one big ear flopped sideways, one eye still a little crusty.

She's a girl. Tiny. Mostly smoke gray with a patch of orange under her chin and white socks on all four paws. Calico, technically, but mostly just scrappy and stubborn.

The exam room door opens. And there he is.

Teddy Abbott.

He stops just short of the threshold. His brows lift, just for a second, but he smooths it over fast. "Well, well," he says, pulling on exam gloves. "We meet again."

He glances at Clara, who peers up at him with her chin tucked behind the kitten bundle.

"What's the emergency?" he asks, voice soft, already stepping forward.

I explain quickly; we found her weak but alert, no mom or litter in sight.

Teddy crouches low in front of Clara. "Let's have a look at this little warrior, huh?" He reaches out carefully, unwrapping the towel layer by layer. The kitten gives a tired little protest mew, blinking blearily up at him. Teddy hums under his breath, murmuring nonsense in that automatic vet voice calming, low. But when Clara doesn't react, he looks up. I see the moment it lands. His hands still. His gaze flicks from Clara to me, not surprised, not awkward. Just... re-calibrating.

Then without a word he adjusts. He signs, clumsily but earnestly, ***"Gentle. Careful."***

Clara's face lights up like someone flipped a switch. She nods hard and signs back, ***"Soft. Mine."***

Teddy chuckles low in his throat and runs a hand gently over the kitten's ragged fur. "She's a mess," he murmurs. "But I've seen worse. She's still got fight in her."

The exam is quick but thorough. Fleas, of course. A little underweight. A healing scratch on one back paw. But no infection, no fever, no broken bones. "She will need good food, lots of fluids, and rest. But she'll pull through."

He looks down at Clara. "You've got yourself a tough one," he says, half-smiling.

Clara presses both hands to her chest and signs, ***"Love!"*** It's big, emphatic, full of truth.

Teddy glances at me. "She's something else."

"Yeah," I say softly. "She is."

We leave with a flea treatment, a bottle of kitten formula, and a handful of instructions scribbled in neat, all-caps block letters. Clara carries the wrapped kitten like she's something precious, and maybe she is.

At the front door, Teddy signs, ***"Bye!"*** awkwardly but with his full chest behind it.

Clara waves back so hard that she almost drops the kitten. I adjust them both before heading back out into the sun. We still have a party to get to.

The ranch hums under the setting sun when we return. Family gathering, food on the tables, swing set leaning slightly in the breeze.

Home.

There were nights not so long ago when I sat on this same porch, staring out at the same dusty yard, and wondered how I was supposed to raise a child alone. But I did it. I built this life. It's not perfect, not easy, but it's ours. After Clara's cake, after the candles and the gifts and the mess, after she's curled up asleep, kitten tucked against her chest, I notice the bracelet Grayson's mom gave her glinting faintly on her wrist.

I sit alone on the porch swing, watching the stars bloom across the sky. I tell myself it's enough, that I don't have time for anything else. But somewhere, deep down, in the quiet spaces between heartbeats,

I wonder if maybe just maybe the story isn't quite finished yet.

Chapter 31
Grayson

The first thing I notice is the ceiling. Smooth. Pale cream paint. No cracks. No water stains. No flickering fluorescent buzz.

Just clean.

I blink hard, the light stabbing against my skull, and roll onto my side. The bed is too soft. The sheets are too crisp. The room smells like lemons and something rich I can't place like a hotel lobby, I'd never be allowed to walk through.

The door clicks open.

I flinch instinctively, pushing up onto my elbows, blinking at the figure that steps inside. Woman. Mid-thirties. Scrubs. Blonde ponytail. She smiles polite but detached and raises her hands. ***"Good morning, Grayson. Welcome to Sunrise Hills."*** Her signing is slow and deliberate better than most I've ever seen outside the band.

I scowl, dragging my palms over my face. My skin itches. My stomach twists. She crosses the room without waiting for permission, presses a thermometer against my temple, and checks my pulse with gentle, practiced fingers. ***"Withdrawal symptoms are normal,"*** she signs casually as if we're discussing the weather.

I yank my arm away when she reaches for the blood pressure cuff.

She smiles. ***"You can hate me all you want. You're still here."***

I flip her off. She pats my knee lightly, infuriatingly, and glides out the door. The following hours, or maybe days, blur. Sweat pools under me, soaking the sheets. The food tray arrives with thick soup, fresh bread, and grilled chicken that is rich, healthy, and smells too good. I shove it off the bedside table.

It crashes to the floor with a satisfying splatter. Someone comes in to clean it up without a word. Without looking at me.

I throw up twice. I shake so badly I can barely control my hands. The nurse, I think her name is Sam, signs quick instructions. ***"Breathe. Sip water. You won't die."***

I glare at her. She shrugs like she's seen a thousand just like me. Probably has. At some point, Jude appears. Crisp suit. Pressed shirt. Not a wrinkle out of place. He stands at the foot of my bed like he's inspecting a very disappointing auction lot.

"Six months," he signs sharply. ***"Minimum."***

I sign something vulgar back.

He barely lifts an eyebrow. ***"Court's ready if you aren't. Stay. Or don't. Your choice."*** He pivots on his heel and walks out like he doesn't have a care in the world, never looking back.

I lose track of time. After two weeks, they move me from the med wing to a "residential suite." That's what they call it, a suite. It feels like a joke. The bed is bigger. The windows are wide, letting in golden afternoon sun. There's even a TV mounted on the wall, muted but flashing cheerful, stupid images. They try to engage me in group sessions, individual therapy, art classes, and yoga. I ignore all of it.

At breakfast, a guy at my table, maybe fifty, bald, shaky, tries to start a conversation. I stare through him. I feel the table vibrate faintly under my elbows as he drums anxious fingers against it. Everywhere I turn, someone's smiling. Encouraging. Fake.

They offer me gourmet meals three times a day: roasted vegetables, seared salmon, and homemade granola bars. I eat mechanically enough to keep the nurses off my back, but the food tastes like sawdust in my mouth anyway. At night, the sheets smell too clean. The silence feels wrong, not full of vibrating basslines or city hum, but dead and heavy. I don't think about the band. Not Jensen, not Delilah, not Knox. I don't think about Jude. I don't think about Maddie. I don't think about anything.

Just the next breath. The next hour. The next goddamn fight to stay upright.

One afternoon, during a mandatory counseling intake, the therapist, a gray-haired woman with kind eyes and a deceptively ruthless signing style, asks me why I'm here.

"Because Jensen Parker's too much of a coward to let me ruin myself in peace," I snap back.

She smiles faintly. *"That's not why."*

I clench my jaw, refusing to answer.

"We'll find the real reason eventually," she signs calmly. It's infuriating. *"You can either fight us... or find yourself."*

I sign back, *"Fuck off,"* with vicious precision.

She only smiles wider.

I dream that night. Not like a story. Not even like a memory. Just fragments. Heat. Pressure. Hands. I'm sweating through the sheets. Shaking. The rhythm is there at first steady, pulsing like the echo of a live show buried under my skin. But then it twists. Slips.

I drop the sticks.

Again and again and again.

They fall through my fingers like they don't belong to me anymore. Like *I* don't belong behind the kit. I lunge to grab them, but my hands don't move fast enough. My arms feel like lead. My pulse chokes in my throat. And Maddie's there. Not her face; I never get to keep her face. Just her hands. And then she's gone. I jolt awake in the dark, gasping, drenched.

My heart's hammering too fast. I press my palm to my chest like that'll slow it down. The silence in the room is crushing. I feel it crawl up my spine. The rhythm's gone. My arms ache like I played a ten-hour set. My hands are fists, and I don't remember making them.

I look at the blanket. Rip it off. Then I throw it. Hard. Across the room. It hits the dresser and slides down like it doesn't care. I swing at the pillow next. Slam it against the floor. The bedside lamp soft, modern, overpriced goes next. It bounces off the edge of the chair and shatters on the tile.

Still not enough.

I grab the wooden tray from the dresser, the one with the glass water bottle and the stupid hand-folded note welcoming me, and hurl it at the door. The water explodes across the wood. The tray splinters. Glass cracks. I stand there in the wreckage, chest heaving, wrists burning, fists clenched so tight they shake.

No one comes. No alarm. No knock. No judgment.

Just me. Just the silence. Just the bitter, twisting shame curling under my ribs where the dream used to be. I sit down on the edge of the bed, panting like I ran a mile. My hands still won't stop shaking. And for the first time since I got here...

I want to cry.

But I don't. I can't. So I stare at the floor, at the broken lamp and scattered glass, and wait for the panic to pass. Because it always does.

Eventually.

Morning comes, whether I want it to or not. The scent of lemon cleaner hangs in the air sharper today, like they scrubbed the room down before I woke up. Like they're trying to erase the mess I made.

The breakfast tray waits just inside the door, perfectly balanced, untouched. I don't remember anyone coming in. The bedside lamp is gone. The broken glass, swept. The water bottle replaced. The tray? New. As if last night didn't happen.

Even the welcome note's been reprinted same script, same lie. Staff walk the halls just beyond the door firm-footed, their movements sending small vibrations through the floorboards. Steady. Predictable. Like this place runs whether I'm in it or not. Because it does.

Life's moving on. And I'm just... here. Sitting on the edge of the bed, sweat-damp T-shirt clinging to my spine, knuckles clenched until they crack like old wood. Everything in this room is too clean. The room is spotless. The mess I made? Erased. Like it never happened. It's too forgiving. This place is too forgiving.

Like it's waiting for me to fall in line. To breathe deep. To start over. But I don't deserve that. I trashed the room. I destroyed their silence.

And they gave me clean sheets and another chance. I sit on the edge of the bed, elbows on my knees, fists digging into my forehead. The floor vibrates under quiet footsteps. Life moves on. I don't know how to. My jaw locks. My teeth grind. I'm not like them. I'm not someone who gets better. I do not earn forgiveness just because the staff here pretend I haven't ruined everything.

I don't get to be clean.

Chapter 32
Maddie

Clara- 3 years old

The morning sun spills across the ranch like liquid gold. The oak trees cast long, dappled shadows over the yard. The air hums warm but not brutal yet the sweet scent of fresh-cut hay drifting from the barn.

Inside the house, chaos reigns. Streamers hang crookedly from the ceiling. Paper plates and plastic cups teeter on the kitchen counters. Mom is elbow-deep in cake batter. Wyatt and Colt argue over how to hang a piñata correctly without losing an eye. And in the middle of it all, Clara. Her curls are wilder this year longer, sun-bleached at the tips. Her tiny paper crown is already askew, and the kitten sleek now, no longer a scrappy ball of fur, circles her ankles, mewing impatiently.

Clara signs, *"Cake?"* with frantic urgency.

I laugh, scooping her into my arms. ***"Not yet, sunshine. You have to wait for the party."***

She signs, ***"Wait,"*** with a melodramatic sigh, throwing herself against my chest.

Outside, the front gate creaks open. A dusty blue truck rumbles up the drive, kicking gravel in slow spirals. I wipe my hands on my jeans and head out with Clara balanced on my hip. Teddy climbs down from the truck bed, toolbox in one hand, an easy grin on his face. He signs, ***"Hi, Clara!"*** He's still slow about it but better than last year. Clara signs back a whole, excited paragraph, which he clearly struggles to keep up with. He chuckles, helpless. "I caught about three words," he says, smiling at me.

"That's about average," I tease, adjusting Clara's crown. "She's got her own language some days." Teddy's here to check on one of Colt's horses, a mild colic scare, but he lingers near the edge of the action afterward, sipping lemonade that Clara proudly "served" him (after mostly spilling half of it down his jeans).

Grayson's parents arrive a few minutes later. They make it a point to fly down twice a year to visit from Texas every year since Clara was born. His mom beelines for Clara, signing, ***"Happy Birthday!"*** with slow, careful hands. Clara beams, throwing her arms around her waist. Grayson's dad trails behind, carrying a battered gift bag and trying to look gruff about it. I catch his face soften the second Clara turns away.

The party hums to life. Luke somehow talks half the ranch hands into a three-legged race. Colt brings out a battered guitar, strumming off-key birthday songs while the kids shriek and run underfoot. The cake wobbles dangerously as Mom brings it out, lopsided but beautiful, frosted with pink and purple swirls. Everyone gathers around the old picnic table. Clara claps her hands excitedly, the goat toy tucked firmly under one arm. We sign the birthday song together, laughter spilling into the warm air, hands moving in messy, perfect rhythm. Clara blows out the candles in one fierce puff. The whole yard cheers. The kitten claws halfway onto the table, trying to steal frosting.

Presents pile up around her: A tiny saddle from Luke "for when she's ready to ride for real."

A pink cowgirl hat from Wyatt and Colt, complete with glittering rhinestones. Handmade storybooks from Grayson's mom, with simple words and bright pictures, that Clara can feel and learn from. And then the kitten decides the ribbon is more important than anything else and stage-dives into the middle of the chaos. I sit back against the fence, watching Clara laugh and sign frantically at everyone around her, no interpreter needed, no slowing down, just pure, wild joy. Three years ago, I sat on this same porch, counting fingers and toes by the moon's pale light, too scared to imagine a future. Today, the future is loud, messy, and beautiful.

Later, after the food's mostly gone and the sun starts to slide low, Teddy drifts over. Clara's passed out in the shade under the oak tree, kitten curled into her side. I brush a hand down my arm, wiping off frosting smudged somewhere between cake-cutting and chaos.

"She's getting so big," Teddy says quietly, nodding toward Clara. "And still probably the cutest thing I've ever seen pass out mid-party."

I smile without meaning to. "She earned it. She's been on a sugar-fueled victory lap since noon."

"She's got your energy," he says. "And your glare when anyone suggested she needed a nap."

That gets a soft laugh from me.

Teddy shifts his weight. "You always throw parties this good, or is this a ranch-only phenomenon?"

"Only for three-year-olds who think goats are royalty," I say, brushing my hair out of my face.

He smiles again, slower this time. "I, uh..." He pauses, then adds, "I was wondering if I could take you out sometime."

I blink, my heart thudding against my ribs. He doesn't make it weird. Doesn't push. He stands there with that easy posture and lets the question hang gently in the quiet between us.

"I should probably say no," I murmur, not quite looking at him. "Schedules. Life. A goat toy currently running my household."

"But," he prompts, hopeful.

"But," I echo, glancing back at Clara in the grass, "I'm not saying no."

He grins, wide and real. "What if it's not a date? Just... coffee. As a thank-you. For the kitten. And the tire."

"Oh, you're pulling the favor card?"

"Shamelessly," he says. "You'd be robbing me of closure if you said no."

I snort. "Closure?"

"Yeah," he says, stepping a little closer. "I fixed your tire. I patched up your stray. All I'm asking is fifteen minutes of caffeine-based gratitude."

"That sounds dangerously like a bribe."

"Technically, it's extortion," he chirps. "But I'm charming, so it sounds better."

I laugh again, shaking my head. "Alright. One coffee."

"As a thank-you," he repeats, holding up his hands like he's innocent.

"Sure," I say, lips twitching. "Let's go with that."

Teddy flashes a satisfied smile and eases down to sit beside me in the grass, not too close, but near enough that I feel his warmth settle at my side. The sun dips lower, casting long, honey-colored shadows across the yard. Laughter carries from the porch quieter now but full of something whole.

Clara's still asleep under the oak, one arm slung over the kitten, goat toy smushed under her cheek like a pillow.

"She always sleep that hard?" Teddy asks beside me, voice soft.

I nod. "When she finally gives in, yeah. The world could fall, and she'd keep dreaming."

He watches her for a beat, then glances at me. "She's... fearless."

I swallow around the sudden tightness in my throat. "She is," I say. "I used to think I had to make her that way. Teach her how to be strong."

"And now?"

"Now, I think she already was. I just had to get out of her way."

Teddy says nothing, but the quiet between us feels like agreement.

I look at Clara again, wild curls tangled, sock half-off, smile barely ghosting her lips, and something settles deep in my chest. She's safe. She's growing. She's everything I never dared to hope for, wrapped in frosting-sticky fingers and second chances.

And for once, I don't feel like I'm waiting for the other shoe to drop.

Chapter 33
Grayson

They don't tell me they're coming. No heads-up. No warning. Just a shift in routine, a new line on the schedule that wasn't there yesterday. Room Three. Private.

The therapist signs it like it's nothing. ***"Visitor request."***

I sign back, slowly, ***"Who?"***

He doesn't answer. Just waits, calm and unreadable. I follow him down the hallway. Feet dragging. Heart pounding. Expecting a sponsor. A donor. Maybe another deaf guy with a guitar and a laminated success story.

Not this.

Not them.

My mother stands the second I walk in. She's gripping her purse strap like it's anchoring her to the floor. Her eyes are bloodshot. Her mouth trembling like she's rehearsed what she'll say a thousand times and still doesn't believe it will land.

And next to her

My father.

Stiff in a chair that's too small for him. Suit wrinkled. Eyes blank. His hands are still. His mouth is a hard line. He doesn't belong here, and he knows it. I freeze in the doorway. The therapist is already seated in the corner. Neutral. Present.

He signs, slow and steady, ***"You don't have to stay."***

I want to bolt. To turn and run until the walls of this place vanish behind me. But I don't.

I sit. And the silence swallows me whole.

Not the easy silence of being deaf. Not the kind that's always been mine. This is a different kind. Heavy. Suffocating. Poisoned. My father stares at the floor. Like I'm too much to look at.

My mother signs first, hands small and careful. ***"You look healthy."***

I don't answer. I don't trust my face not to crack. The therapist watches me. No pressure. No judgment.

Then my father speaks. He does not sign. He speaks. The words come from his mouth, not his hands, and they hit harder because of it. The therapist signs alongside him, slow and clean.

"I thought you should know the truth," he says. "It may help fix what I broke."

I tense. My nails dig into my palms.

"You were five. It was my fault."

Everything in me goes rigid.

"You were playing hide and seek. You climbed into the trunk of the car. I didn't know."

The therapist hesitates, just slightly, then keeps going.

"I was drinking. I was yelling. I got in the car. I didn't check the back."

There's no memory. No flash of recognition.

Only cold. I remember the hospital. The bandages. The quiet. My mother's hands. But not the car.

Not the crash. Not him.

"You pushed through the seat halfway down the road," he says. "I saw your face in the mirror. And I swerved." He stops. Swallows. Then "The car rolled. I lost control. We hit the ditch and flipped."

I suck in a breath that claws its way down my throat. My hands are white-knuckled in my lap. I don't feel them anymore. Only pressure.

"You hit your head," he says. "The doctors said the trauma... it was too much. It cost you everything."

I stare at him. Then at her.

My mother signs, hands trembling: ***"You never remembered. And we didn't want to give you another wound to carry."***

My jaw locks.

"You watched him walk through that door every day," I sign, stiff and sharp, ***"and you let me believe he was tired."***

My father flinches.

"You let me build a life on a lie."

He nods, eyes glassy. "After the crash, I went to jail. Then rehab." He glances around the room, bitter. "Funny, right?"

"When I came home, I didn't know how to be a father. I didn't know how to face you. But I worked. I threw everything I had at making sure you had a shot at being normal. The best doctors. The best schools. The best specialists. I figured... if I couldn't be what you needed, maybe I could buy it."

"And still," I sign, my fingers shaking now, ***"you let me grow up thinking I was born broken. You let me believe this silence was mine, that it was who I was, not something someone ripped away from me."***

His head drops. "I thought if you didn't remember, maybe... maybe you wouldn't hate me."

My mother signs softly, barely holding it together, ***"He couldn't live with what he did, but he stayed. He tried. He never forgave himself, and neither did I."***

"But you still chose to keep it from me," I sign, the shape of each word jagged and violent. ***"You built my whole life around not telling me who I really am."***

She flinches. Then signs, ***"We thought if we told you... It would shatter what little peace you had left."***

I want to scream. I want to punch a wall. Or break something. Or rewind time. But I just sit there. Burning in silence. Because now I know the truth.

And it doesn't fix anything.

It just makes the wreck real. Like it's still happening. Like, I'm still five. Stuck in the dark. Waiting to be found.

They leave.

I stay.

And I count every breath like it might be the one that finally breaks me. The next day, I skip breakfast. Stay in my room. Try to write. Rip the pages up. Try again. Everything inside my skull feels too loud. Everything outside feels too quiet.

I don't know who I am anymore. Not really. If I wasn't born this way, if the silence wasn't part of me from the start, then what am I? Just a story someone else wrote. A lie I've been performing my whole life. When someone rings the flashing bell, I almost don't answer.

The staff signs, ***"Visitor."***

My stomach knots. I brace for my mother.

But it's Mia.

She doesn't wave. Doesn't throw her arms around me. She just walks in slowly and sits across from me on the bench. Her face is tired. Her eyes steady. We sit in silence.

Five minutes. Maybe more.

Then she signs, fluid but blunt, ***"You look like shit."***

I almost laugh. Almost.

I sign back, ***"You flew out here just to tell me that?"***

She shakes her head and signs, ***"I came because no one else had the guts to."***

I raise an eyebrow.

She shrugs. ***"And because... I owe you the truth."***

I wait.

She exhales, picking at a frayed thread on her jeans. ***"I used to be jealous of you."***

I blink.

She keeps going. ***"You were born different. But you made it look easy. Like being deaf didn't stop you. Like music still lives in you no matter what. And I"***

She swallows. ***"I had to fight for every inch of myself. My parents didn't want this. Music. Touring. The band. It was a war. Still is."***

Her signing slows but never falters. She's fluent, but this part isn't rehearsed. It's raw.

I study her.

She continues, *"You had something I didn't. You were seen and valued, not just for what you could do but for who you were."*

I sign slower than before. *"My dad never looked at me for years."*

Mia shakes her head. *"But your mom did. She stayed, fought for you, and loved you for more than what you gave back."*

There's bitterness in her expression. But also grief. She doesn't elaborate. She doesn't have to. I reach out. We hug. No theatrics. No sudden fix. Just two people finally letting themselves be held.

When she leaves, she signs, *"Keep breathing."*

And I nod. Because for the first time in forever, I might want to. That afternoon, I go back to Room Three. The therapist is waiting.

He signs, *"Do you want to talk about it?"*

I sit down. My hands are unsteady. My stomach is tight. But I look him in the eye.

And I sign back, *"Yeah. I do."*

Chapter 34
Maddie

The house is still.

Sunlight filters through the curtains in soft gold stripes, casting warmth over the tangled blankets and the curve of a man's shoulder beside me.

Teddy's here.

He doesn't stay often. We've never made that leap, but sometimes, like last night, it's just easier. Clara had a nightmare. The storm knocked out power for half an hour. And before I could overthink it, he'd offered to crash on the couch.

He didn't make it to the couch.

Now he's stretched out beside me, one arm folded under his head, the other resting lightly on the bedspread like he's afraid to touch too much. I blink sleep from my eyes and shift my hand, and that's when I feel it.

Cold metal. My breath catches. There, resting on my left ring finger is a ring. Simple. Elegant. A delicate solitaire on a thin gold band.

I go still.

And that's when I realize Teddy's already watching me. Propped up on one elbow. Quiet. Steady.

His smile is soft. Nervous. "Morning."

I glance down at the ring. Then back at him. "Teddy...?"

He shrugs, the barest movement. "I didn't want a big moment. No speeches. No grand gestures. Just... this."

He watches me like he's bracing for impact. "You don't have to say yes. You don't even have to keep it. I just..." He pauses. "I love you. And I love her. And this already feels like home. I just wanted to ask if I could stay."

My throat tightens. Outside, I hear Clara in the hallway humming off-key, goat toy thumping against the wall as she runs past the door.

I look at Teddy.

At the ring.

At this soft, steady life, we've built. No fireworks, no dramatics. Just mornings like this. I nod. His breath catches.

"Yes," I whisper. "You can stay."

He smiles so wide it crinkles the corners of his eyes. Then he leans down and kisses me slowly, surely, like he's been waiting his whole life for this one. Teddy helps me make breakfast while Clara clomps in her mismatched socks, still clutching her stuffed goat like it's security clearance for the kitchen.

She notices the ring. Stops mid-step.

Her eyes go wide, and she signs, *"New?"* Then, more excited, *"Pretty!"*

I nod and smile tightly. ***"Yes. Teddy asked if he could stay forever."***

Clara tilts her head, thinking. Then she signs, serious and simple, ***"He's already ours."***

I blink fast. My heart pulls tight.

Teddy kneels beside her, brushing a curl back from her face. He signs slowly, ***"I would love to be yours. Always."***

Clara beams. Then signs, ***"Okay. But waffles first. I pick!"***

Clara's fourth birthday falls on a Saturday. The weather holds warm and dry, with just enough breeze to keep the decorations from sagging. Ribbons whip lightly around the porch railings. Mom's already set out half a dozen dishes too early. Wyatt's building something near the barn that looks suspiciously like a goat obstacle course.

Teddy moves around the backyard like he's always been here, like he grew out of the soil. He helps Colt hang the piñata, distracts Clara when she gets too close to the candles, and signs, ***"Careful,"*** with a playful little shake of his head.

Clara signs back, ***"Bossy,"*** but she's grinning.

It's everything I never thought I'd have. The sound of tires crunching gravel has me turning toward the drive. Grayson's parents step out of the car slowly. His mom carries a small, wrapped box, and his dad wears his discomfort like a too-tight suit.

Clara doesn't hesitate.

She spots them and takes off running, curls bouncing, goat tucked under one arm like a football. His mother crouches without hesitation. Clara barrels into her arms, signs, *"Hi!"* fast and bright, and then immediately holds up her toy.

Grayson's mom signs back gently, *"He looks hungry."*

Clara nods seriously. His dad stands stiffly at the edge of the yard, hands in his pockets, eyes locked on Clara like she might vanish if he blinks. I walk over to him, heart tight.

"Thanks for coming," I say.

He nods, barely. Swallows. His voice cracks when he finally says, "She's getting so big."

I glance at her arms waving as she explains something in fast, messy signs. "She is," I say softly. "She's happy."

He nods again. Doesn't speak. Eventually, Clara trots over to him, grabs his hand, and tugs him toward the cake table.

He follows.

Grayson's mom slips beside me, her eyes tracking Clara. *"She's so much like him,"* she says. *"Same eyes. Same stubborn chin."*

I nod, blinking hard. We stand together in silence, watching Grayson's father let Clara lead him through a world he clearly doesn't understand.

"He didn't know how to be a father," she signs eventually. *"But he's trying now. Because of her."*

I glance sideways, throat tight. *"She's good at giving people second chances."*

Grayson's mom looks at me and then touches my arm. *"He's not the only one trying."*

I freeze.

She studies me. Then signs, *"You should know where he is."*

My stomach drops.

"He's in rehab. A private one. Has been for over a year now."

I can't breathe. *"Why didn't anyone tell me?"*

"He didn't want you to know. Not until he was ready."

Her gaze softens. *"But I think... You deserve the truth. Especially after everything you gave up."*

My hands shake. I curl them into fists and look away.

"He's working hard," she signs. *"Really hard. You gave him that push, Maddie. Whether you meant to or not."*

I swallow hard. Clara laughs in the distance a quiet, open-mouthed burst of happiness as her hands clap. Grayson's father lifts her up and twirls her around, awkward but careful. She signs, *"Again!"* Fast and eager.

Grayson's mom signs, ***"You gave her the best parts of him. And now you're giving them back to us."***

Clara picks out the biggest piece of cake and insists on giving it to Grayson's dad. He takes it with both hands like it might fall apart if he doesn't. And for a moment, just one beat in this wild, complicated life, I see what it might look like if none of us were broken.

If we were just family.

Chapter 35

Grayson

The halfway house is quiet in the mornings.

No slamming doors. No yelling. No staff tapping on your shoulder just to get your attention. Just sunlight through cheap blinds and the muted shuffle of movement through walls I can't hear. I sit on the edge of the twin bed and flex my fingers like I'm warming up to drum again.

I haven't touched a kit in over a year. Not since Jude brought me through the front doors of that clean, white rehab center eighteen months ago with a signed intake form and a face full of guilt. I didn't think I'd make it a week.

Now I'm here.

Signing transition paperwork. Talking to staff about job leads. Housing options. Building a life from rubble. I pull on my hoodie, slower than usual, like the movement might hold me together.

The light from the doorbell flashes just after. I glance up. A familiar shape behind the frosted glass.

I open the door. It's my mom.

She smiles soft, unsure, and signs, *"Can I come in?"*

I nod and step aside. She takes in the room like she's never been here before, though I know she helped set it up. She doesn't sit right away.

Finally, she signs, *"You look good."*

I shrug.

She nods slowly. Then signs again, *"I talked to your counselors before I came."*

That gets my attention. My spine straightens. *"Why?"*

Her hands move carefully, deliberately, and unsure. *"Because there's something I need to tell you. Something you deserve to know."*

I wait.

She swallows hard. *"You have a daughter."*

The words don't land. Not at first. Not really.

I blink.

"Her name is Clara."

My whole body locks up.

"What are you talking about?" I sign, sharp. *"Who? Maddie?"*

My mother nods her head, sadness etched into every line of her face. *"She didn't know where you were. For a long time, none of us did. She only found out a few months ago that you were here, safe, getting help."*

I stare at her, barely breathing. *"Why didn't you tell me?"*

She hesitates. Then, *"Because you were using. And Maddie was scared. I was afraid you'd relapse if you found out too soon. Frightened you wouldn't be able to handle it."* She pulls out her phone, taps a few times, and then turns the screen toward me. A little girl fills the frame. Blonde curls. Blue eyes. A tiny goat plushie clutched in one hand. Her smile is small but real. Determined.

Something in me cracks. A slow, splintering break.

"She's deaf," my mom signs. *"Just like me, just like you."*

I reach for the phone like it might slip away. Stare hard enough to memorize her. *"She's five?"* I sign, even though I already know the answer.

"Yes," she signs. *"Maddie didn't want to hide her from you. She was just trying to protect her."*

"You all kept her from me," I sign, anger pushing through the shock. *"For five years. Because I wasn't perfect?"*

My mother's face crumples. *"Because you weren't ready."*

"You don't get to decide that," I sign, each motion sharp and vicious. *"That was my daughter. My choice. And I've missed everything."*

She steps back like I hit her. I turn away. ***"You should go,"*** I sign without looking.

She lingers in the doorway. Then signs, ***"She deserves to know you. And you deserve to know her. When you're ready."***

I say nothing. She leaves. I sit there until the light through the blinds shifts, and my hands stop shaking. Then I grab my jacket and start walking. Not toward anything.

Just... away.

Eventually, I find myself on a bench outside a church. The air is crisp. My lungs feel too tight in my chest. The world feels too still for what's just been undone inside me.

I text Jude: *Need to talk.*

Fifteen minutes later, he's there. No questions. Just sits.

I sign, ***"I have a daughter."***

Jude's eyes widen, but only for a second. Then he lets out a long breath, nods slowly, and signs, ***"Yeah. I know."***

I blink. ***"You knew?"***

He shrugs. ***"Your mom reached out. Months ago. Wanted advice. I told her to wait until you were steady. Until you could hear it without falling apart."***

"And you agreed with that?" I sign, heat rising up my throat.

"No, " he signs, steady. ***"But I also knew you'd spiral if you found out back then. You weren't ready. You wanted to die. Don't pretend you didn't."***

My jaw clenches. My whole chest is coiled.

Jude watches me. Calm. Real. ***"But you're here now. You're stronger now. You didn't lose everything, Grayson. You still get to choose what kind of father you want to be."***

I bury my face in my hands. My palms go damp.

He waits until I look back up. Then signs, ***"You're allowed to be angry. But don't stay stuck there. She's real. She's yours. And you're not that kid in the dark anymore."***

Something in me stutters. *You're not that kid in the dark anymore.*

The words land deep.

Jude leans back on the bench, eyes on the street. ***"We'll figure it out. One thing at a time."*** And so we sit.

Breathing. One beat at a time.

That night, Jude gets us takeout in big paper bags smelling like garlic and regret. Without a word, he sets it all down on the rickety table in the common room. I sit across from him, appetite flickering in and out like my body can't decide whether it's running on grief or adrenaline.

I open one of the containers. Pasta. Extra cheese. I poke at it with the plastic fork like it might bite me first. Finally I sign, *"She likes goats."*

Jude grins, chewing. *"You saw the plushie."*

I nod. *"She looked happy."*

"She is," he signs. *"Maddie's done a good job."*

I stare at my plate. Then, *"She didn't deserve to do it alone."*

Jude doesn't argue. Just keeps eating.

I sign again, *"What do I have to do to see her? What's the process?"*

He wipes his hands. Leans back. *"You're already doing it. Stay clean. Keep going to group. Show the board you can hold a job, pay rent, and maintain stability. You're close."*

"Close isn't enough," I sign. *"I've missed five years."*

"So don't miss six," he signs, **"simple."**

It cuts deep.

I exhale and sign slower now, *"What if she doesn't want to meet me?"*

Jude pauses. *"Then you keep showing up. You keep trying. And one day, maybe... she lets you in. But even if she doesn't,"* he leans forward, *"you keep being the kind of man worth knowing. Also, apologize to your mother."*

My throat tightens. I nod once. The pasta's gone cold, but I eat it anyway. It's the first time food has tasted like something other than shame. And for the first time in months, I feel like I'm not just trying to stay alive.

I'm trying to live.

Chapter 36
Maddie

The sun is hot against my back as I latch the gate near the horse paddock. My arms ache, sweat slicks my neck, and I've got mud on my knees from fixing a busted trough line. It's been a long morning. I'm halfway through brushing the grit off my jeans when I feel a strange shift in the air, a pressure, a presence.

I turn. He's standing at the edge of the path.

Grayson.

My breath catches. He looks... older. Thinner. But steadier than I've seen him in a long time. There's something behind his eyes now, something quieter, more still.

And suddenly, I can't move. He lifts his hands. ***"Hey."***

My fingers twitch at my sides. It takes a beat before I can lift them. ***"What are you doing here?"***

"I needed to see you," he signs.

My heart thuds hard. ***"You can't just show up."***

"I didn't come to make trouble," he signs. *"I found out about Clara."*

I flinch. My whole body goes tight.

"My mom told me," he adds. *"She showed me a picture."*

I look away. The wind catches my hair, and I don't push it back. My hands shake when I sign, *"You were using. You didn't remember, but the next morning, it was me. It was us. Then again, at the party, we were both not sober."*

I swallow. The words ache. *"I didn't tell you because I was trying to protect her. I didn't even know where you were until a few months ago."*

His expression twists. He steps forward. *"You should've told me,"* he signs. *"The moment you knew."*

I snap. My fingers fly, furious and shaking. *"You think I didn't want to? Do you think this hasn't eaten me alive? You were gone, Grayson. You were high and spiraling and completely unreachable. Do you think I wanted this? Do you think I wanted to raise a baby alone? To work two jobs just to afford diapers while you were God knows where? Do you think I wanted to move back with my parents and live in my old bedroom? I didn't have the luxury of running. I stayed. I built something stable so she'd never have to wonder if someone was coming back."* My chest rises and falls too fast. *"I had to choose. I chose her."*

"She's my daughter," he signs.

"She's my whole world," I fire back. ***"And I wasn't going to let you shatter her just because you didn't know how to hold yourself together."***

We're both trembling, words slashing the space between us. And then a car door slams.

I freeze.

Footsteps.

No. Not now. I turn, panic blooming in my chest. Teddy rounds the corner of the barn, Clara's hand in his. She's wearing her pink jacket and muddy boots, goat plushie tucked under one arm. She's signing something excitedly, probably about the chickens, while bouncing on her toes.

Then she sees him.

The man in the hoodie with shadows under his eyes. She stops. So does Teddy.

His gaze flicks from me to Grayson. Clara tilts her head, curious. Her blue eyes land on Grayson really land. Like something about him calls to something in her. My heart stutters.

Grayson stares at her like the world just cracked open.

And I don't know whether to run or fall to my knees. Teddy steps forward first. His voice is calm, but his posture is tension-filled. "Hey," he says, offering a cautious smile. "I'm Teddy. You must be..."

Grayson lifts his hands and signs, *"Grayson."*

Teddy falters for half a second, then switches smoothly to sign. *"Nice to meet you."*

Grayson nods once, still watching Clara.

She edges closer to Teddy's side, her little fingers flicking fast. *"Who is that?"*

Teddy glances at me, uncertain.

I step forward. My hands are steadier than I feel. *"Clara, this is... this is Grayson. He came to see me today."*

She frowns a little, curious. I crouch in front of her, brushing her curls from her face. *"Why don't you go inside with Teddy and get ice cream? Just one. You earned it today."*

Clara's eyes light up. She signs *"Really?"* and I nod. *"Yes. Just one."*

She grabs Teddy's hand without hesitation and starts tugging him toward the house. Grayson's eyes follow her not just to Clara, but to her hand in Teddy's. The way she leans into his side. The way she signs to him like it's normal, natural, safe.

When I stand back up, I see his eyes locked on my left hand.

The ring.

His jaw clenches. Shoulders stiff. He doesn't say anything.

But then his hands move. *"So that's it?"* He signs. *"You moved on, built a life without me, and I don't even get a say."*

I stare at him. *"What were you expecting? That I'd wait forever? That I'd freeze time until you decided to come back?"*

"She's mine." His signs are hard and clipped. *"And he gets to be in the house. At the table. He gets the questions and the giggles and the bedtime stories."*

"Because he stayed," I cut in, my signs just as sharp. *"Because he showed up when it mattered. Because I didn't have to wonder if he'd come back when things got hard."*

His arms drop to his sides, eyes looking to the porch like it might offer answers. *"I didn't know,"* he signs after a long moment. *"I didn't know she existed. And now... I don't even know where I stand."*

I take a breath. It shudders out of me. My fingers slow. *"Then start here,"* I sign. *"Start by standing by, not disappearing again."*

Chapter 37
Grayson

I don't follow them inside. My feet stay rooted in the dirt, and if I move, I might shatter. The porch isn't far, but it feels miles away, like everything good lives just beyond some invisible wall I don't have the right to cross.

I watch the door. Clara's silhouette flits past the window, bright and small, a streak of pink and curls. I feel a weight in my chest. That pull toward something I didn't even know I was missing until five minutes ago.

Maddie's beside me, arms crossed tight. She's watching the house, not me. But I can tell she's still wound up.

I finally lift my hands. ***"Is she always like that? Happy?"***

Maddie's eyes flick toward me, softer than I expected. ***"Yeah. She's joyful. Curious. Thinks the world's made of magic and mud puddles."***

I smile, just barely. It hurts. ***"She signs like she was born doing it."***

"She was." Maddie's expression shifts. *"She's **deaf. Since birth. Like you and your mom. She's never known any-thing else."***

"She's *never had to feel alone,"* I sign. ***"You made sure of that."***

Her lips press together. Not a smile. But not anger either. Just a glint of something unspoken behind her eyes.

"Why didn't you tell me?"

She sighs. Not loud. Just visible, a long breath, chest lifting and falling before her hands move again. ***"You were high when I found out. Then you were gone. No number. No for-warding address. And I didn't have the energy to chase a ghost."*** Her signs slow. ***"Even if I had found you... You weren't in a place to be anyone's father, Grayson. You weren't safe."***

I don't fight that. I can't.

"I would've tried."

Maddie looks at me, really looks. ***"I know. And I would've wanted to believe in that. But love isn't always safe. And Clara deserved better than a maybe."***

The door opens. Teddy steps out again, this time alone. He walks down the steps, his movements steady, protective, and calm.

"Sherbet," he signs when he reaches us. *"Rainbow. Two scoops. She grinned like she had won the lottery."*

Maddie gives a slight nod. He glances at me. *"You staying?"*

I nod. *"If I'm allowed."*

Teddy tilts his head. *"You showed up. That's something."* Then, to Maddie he adds, *"I'll let her color for a bit. You two talk."*

He walks back in without waiting for a reply. I stare after him for a second. *"She thinks he's her dad?"*

"No." Maddie's reply is firm. *"She knows he's Teddy. She knows he loves her. She knows she's mine. That's all she's needed until now."*

I nod slowly. *"What's she like? Does she like all animals or just goats? Stories? Does she hate broccoli? What's her favorite color?"*

Maddie's shoulders ease slightly as she signs, *"She loves goats. Draws them constantly. She hates carrots. Pink is her whole personality. She signs in her sleep sometimes."*

That last part hits harder than it should. *"She sounds... incredible."*

Maddie watches me. *"She is."*

I take a breath. *"Rehab was eighteen months. I spent the first two weeks in a med wing. Then I got moved to a suite.*

Then the halfway house. I've been clean since the day Jude walked me in."

Her brows raise. *"Jude? Jensen's lawyer, Jude?"*

I nod. *"He didn't walk away. I don't know why."*

Maddie blinks slowly like she's trying to piece that version of my life together. *"He must have seen something you didn't yet."*

I look at her, my fingers tight at my sides. Then I finally sign, *"I want to know her. I want to earn whatever space I'm allowed in her life."*

She doesn't answer right away. Then her hands rise. *"Then start by showing up. Staying. Letting her set the pace."*

"I can do that."

"Good."

Her hands drop to her sides, and for the first time since I arrived, she doesn't look like she's trying to protect herself from me. *"Because if you vanish again, I'm not the one you'll be disappointing."*

I nod. *"I won't."*

The sun's lower now, slanting gold across the fields as I return to the truck. My boots drag. My hands ache. There's dirt under my nails and sweat dried along the collar of my shirt, but it's nothing compared to the weight in my chest.

Clara is inside that house. And I'm driving away from her.

For now. The hotel in town is a squat brick building with a busted ice machine and a crooked sign, but I don't care. It's not rehab. It's not the halfway house. It's just a place to sleep. Somewhere I can be still.

Jude's waiting by the front entrance, arms crossed, phone in hand. He straightens when he sees me. Doesn't smile. Doesn't need to.

I simply sign, *"I saw her."*

He nods once. *"And?"*

"She's perfect. deaf. Confident. Five years old. And already full of fire."

He tilts his head. *"You okay?"*

I shake my head. *"Not even close. But I want to be. I want to figure this out."*

Jude claps me on the shoulder. *"Good. Because I got you a room here for the night."*

My brows lift. He shrugs. *"Figured you'd try to sleep in your truck. You're not doing that anymore."*

"I could've"

"I know. But you didn't." He pulls a key card from his pocket and passes it over. *"Room 202. Already checked in."*

I take it, stunned. *"Thanks."*

"Don't thank me yet." His mouth lifts slightly. *"You've got an apartment too. Lease signed. Ten minutes from Maddie's place."*

I blink. *"Wait. What?"*

"I've been working on it for a while. Just needed to know if you'd come." He pauses. *"It'll be furnished by next week. You'll stay here until it's ready."*

I stare at him. *"Why are you doing all this?"*

Jude's signs are calm and straightforward. *"Because Jensen would've. Because I believe in you."*

He pauses. *"And because that little girl deserves a dad who shows up."*

My throat goes tight.

"You start fresh tomorrow, Grayson. Don't waste it."

Chapter 38
Maddie

I watch Grayson walk away.

He doesn't look back. Just rounds the corner of the barn, shoulders hunched, head down like the weight of everything he just learned is pulling him into the earth. I grip the porch rail, nails digging in. There's a throb at the base of my throat, a phantom ache like I'm watching something slip away that I never let myself hope for.

I don't move. Don't breathe. Just stand there while everything inside me folds in. The porch creaks behind me. Teddy steps out, his face unreadable. His arms are folded loosely, but I recognize a tension in his jaw. Not anger exactly, more like restraint. Like he's waiting for me to say the wrong thing and trying not to show how badly he doesn't want to hear it.

"You okay?" he asks.

I nod. Then I shake my head. Then shrug because I don't know what I am.

He walks over and gives me a beat to speak. I don't. "Do you want to tell me everything now?"

I swallow, throat tight. For a second, I consider lying. Spinning it into something easier. But Teddy deserves the truth. All of it. I nod again. "Yeah."

So I do. I tell him everything. About the tour. The nights. The pills. The second time, when we were both not sober. The moment I knew, it was already too late to turn back. How Grayson disappeared. How I didn't try that hard to find him because deep down, I knew the version of him I loved wasn't the one who'd come back. If he ever did.

Teddy listens. Still. Silent. Like if he moves, he might break something. I keep talking, my voice barely above a whisper, watching his eyes dull with each new truth. When I finish, he presses his lips together and looks away, as if he meets my gaze, it might make it real.

"That hurts," he says.

"I know."

He nods. Then leans forward, pressing a kiss to my forehead. "I need a minute."

I let him walk away. Inside, I wash my hands and wipe the sweat off my neck. I sit at the table while Clara finishes her drawing, her lips moving in a silent rhythm like she's imagining music only she can feel, unaware that her world is tilting.

When she runs off to show her picture to my dad, I pull out my phone and text Jensen.

Me: *Hey. Did you know Jude helped Grayson get clean?*

It takes a few minutes.

Jensen: *Jude was always in contact. I haven't heard from Grayson in years, but Mia has.*

So I text Mia.

Me: *I saw him. Today. Grayson.*

Mia: *He's there?* She texts back immediately.

Me: *Yeah. Looks older. Quieter. Still figuring it out.*

Mia: *That sounds about right.*

I hesitate. Then I type. Me: *What do I even do with that?*

Mia's reply comes quick.

Mia: *You don't read a book backward. That chapter of your life is closed. Stop flipping pages looking for a different ending. Start a new one. Whatever that looks like.*

I stare at the screen, her words sinking in slowly. The kind of advice that lands deeper than you'd expect. That makes you sit back and feel everything you've been avoiding. My hands shake a little as I set the phone down. The porch light hums faintly behind me as I step outside. I sit on the swing, pull my knees to my chest, and watch the stars blink to life one by one.

A creak at the screen door pulls my attention.

Clara steps out, barefoot and clutching her drawing. She climbs onto the swing beside me and leans against my arm.

"I made a picture," she signs, pressing it into my lap.

It's us—me, Clara, and Teddy. A house. A goat. A sun in the corner. But there's a fourth figure. Vague. Off to the side. No name.

I trace the lines of the drawing, throat thick. ***"Who's this?"*** I sign.

Clara shrugs. ***"I don't know. He was just... there."***

I hug her close, the stars blurring behind my lashes. Clara leans into me a while longer before I carry her inside. She's half-asleep before I finish signing our goodnight routine, her goat plushie tucked under one arm. I pull the blanket up to her chin, press a kiss on her curls, and turn off the lamp.

Just as the house settles into stillness, I hear a car pull into the driveway.

Teddy.

He comes up the steps slowly, his keys jangling faintly. He doesn't knock; he just pushes the door open and stands there, looking at me like he's still sorting through too many things.

"I'm not going anywhere," he says.

I nod.

"But I need time to catch up to all of this."

"I know."

He sits beside me on the couch, not touching but close. And for now, that's enough.

Teddy drifts off not long after. One arm slung across his chest, breathing slow and even. I watch him momentarily, then slide gently out from under the blanket and rise from the couch. The kitchen is dim, and the only light comes from the microwave clock. I pour a glass of water and lean against the counter.

My phone buzzes.

Unknown number: *Thank you. For today. For not shutting the door. For Clara.*

I stare at the message, thumb hovering over the screen.

Another buzz.

Unknown number: *I don't know what comes next, but I want to try. I want to do better.*

I swallow, set the phone on the counter, and let my fingers wrap tight around the edge of the sink. He's trying. He's late, messy, and full of unknowns. But he's here.

I pick the phone up again.

Me: *I'm glad you're doing better.*

Me: *And for the record... I still can't look at a goat without hearing you say they have chaos in their souls.*

I don't say more. Just press send and let the silence settle around me like something that could be peace.

Chapter 39

Grayson

It's been three months.

Three months since I stood at the edge of the paddock with the kind of weight in my chest that could cave a person in. Since Clara looked up at me with big blue eyes and didn't say anything, but didn't run either.

Now she signs my name like it's always been there.

I see her once every week, sometimes more. I take her to school on Wednesdays, and she shows me the artwork pinned to the classroom walls like it's a gallery exhibit. She signs fast, full of color and curiosity, never missing a beat. Sometimes she calls me Grayson. Sometimes she just signs you. I don't push it.

My apartment is just off Elm, close enough to the bakery to smell cinnamon in the morning. The job's good. I never pictured myself working on a ranch. Hard work, early starts, no one expecting small talk. I like that. Jude checks in once a week. Jensen more often now that he knows I'm not going anywhere.

My parents came by last weekend. My mom brought cookies. My dad didn't say much, just watched Clara and me with a look I couldn't quite read. But he stayed. He watched her sign. He watched me answer. He didn't leave early.

It's progress.

This morning, I'm fixing the latch on the feed room door. It's rusty and crooked, the same as it's been for weeks. Clara's perched on an upturned bucket behind me, goat plushie in her lap, feet swinging in the dust. She's telling me a story, something about the goat being a secret superhero. Her hands move fast, and she's expressive and full of little facial quirks that crack me up.

I smile without thinking.

It's not the kind of smile I used to fake for cameras. It's a real one. The kind that means something. I catch movement out of the corner of my eye and glance toward the barn door.

Maddie.

She's watching us. For a second, she doesn't move. Then she steps back, quiet, careful. I don't try to stop her. Don't chase after her. She gave me this. And I'm not going to waste it.

I kept busy after Maddie walked out. Pretended I didn't keep checking the barn doors. Now I'm out in the pasture, trying not to let her silence sit too long.

The cattle are jumpy today.

We're running a health check, keeping things steady, but one of the bulls isn't having it. He jerks against the gate, snorts, eyes wild. Maddie's on horseback, signing something urgently, too far for me to see clearly. Whatever it is, I know the rhythm of panic when I see it.

But I feel it. Something's wrong. I glance past the fencing, past the gates

Clara.

She's in the field near the old grain bin, crouched in the grass, setting up what looks like a picnic for her stuffed goat. She hasn't noticed the bull. She hasn't noticed anything.

Panic floods my chest so fast I can't think. I take a step forward. Then Maddie rides closer and lifts her arm. She's holding something. A remote.

Clara's bracelet starts flashing. Bright blue light pulses at her wrist.

She sees it. Looks up. And then she sees the bull.

I watch her bolt, small legs pumping, arms tight around her goat. She darts into the nearby equipment shed, slamming the door behind her as the bull kicks up dirt and veers away.

My knees almost give out. I find Maddie first.

My hands are already flying, every motion sharp with panic. ***"What the hell was that?"*** I demand. ***"She was in the field. With a bull loose. What were you thinking?"***

Maddie dismounts, calm but firm. She signs back just as fast, *"She's fine. The bracelet worked."*

"You call that fine? That could've been" But I can't finish it.

"That's why she wears it, Grayson." Maddie's hands are gentler now. *"It vibrates. It lights up. It's for both of you. You can't hear someone yell. She can't either. This keeps her safe."* Maddie steps closer. *"If something's wrong or she's not paying attention, she knows that signal means get somewhere safe. And she did."*

I breathe hard, my chest still heaving. My hands won't stop shaking. *"She's five. She's deaf. She shouldn't have to..."*

"She's deaf," Maddie cuts in, *"not helpless. And this is her home. Her world. She's growing up on a ranch. She has to know how to navigate it, and we teach her how. That bracelet's a tool. Just like any other."*

I close my eyes. All I could think about was losing her. Again. Without ever really getting her.

Maddie places a hand on my arm. *"You were scared. I get it. But she knew what to do. That's what matters."*

I nod slowly. Then I turn toward the shed. She's sitting inside on an old upturned bucket, goat plushie in her lap, kicking her boots softly against the floor.

"Hi," she signs, like nothing happened. *"You okay?"*

I crouch down in front of her, trying to catch my breath. *"I should be asking you that."*

Clara shrugs. *"Ferdinand's just grumpy. He doesn't like needles. I wasn't too close."*

"You ran fast."

"That's what the bracelet means. Flashing light means run safe." She taps her wrist, matter-of-fact.

I blink, throat tight. *"Were you scared?"* I ask.

She tilts her head. *"No. I knew what to do."*

And that's what breaks me. Because she's five. And braver than I've ever been. I reach forward, pulling her into a hug. She lets me. Small arms wrap around my neck, and her cheek presses against my shoulder.

"I'm really glad you're okay," I sign.

She pulls back, smiles, and signs, *"You worry a lot."*

I laugh, silent but real. *"Yeah,"* I sign back. *"I do."*

Later, as the sky turns soft with evening light, I head for my truck. It's been a long day, and my body aches in all the usual places. I'm unlocking the door when a flicker of motion catches in my peripheral vision.

Clara.

She's hugging her goat plushie tight against her chest, brows pinched like she's working up the courage for something big.

I kneel so we're eye level.

She fidgets, then slowly signs, ***"Are you my dad?"***

My breath catches. She watches me, eyes wide. Waiting.

I swallow, my hands heavy as they lift. ***"Yeah."***

Her lips press together. She shifts on her feet. ***"Where were you?"*** she signs.

God.

I glance down, then back at her. ***"I was sick for a while,"*** I sign slowly. ***"But I'm better now. And I'm not going anywhere. Ever again."***

She stares at me for a long moment. Then she drops her goat and throws her arms around my neck.

"I always wanted a dad," she signs against my shoulder.

And I break. Not loud. Just quietly, like something opening inside me I didn't know I still had.

Chapter 40
Maddie

Three months have passed, and things should feel settled by now. But they don't.

Teddy's been quieter lately. He's not cold, just distant. It's like something is building behind his eyes, and he doesn't know what to say. Clara had asked him to braid her hair that morning, something he used to do without hesitation. He fumbled this time, and when I offered to help, he gave me a tight smile and said, "She'll be fine."

But her braids came loose before lunch. It starts as a small comment over coffee. Something about Grayson fixing a fence that wasn't broken. Maybe he should focus on his place instead of being here so much.

I let it slide. Then it comes up again, sharper, after Clara's asleep. "He's always here, Maddie. You don't see it, but he's working his way in."

"He's helping," I say. "And Clara likes having him around."

Teddy leans against the counter, arms folded. "I get that. But when are we going to talk about the wedding? Or are you waiting for him to walk you down the aisle too?"

That one cuts. Because I don't have an answer. Because I haven't been planning. Not really. I've been circling the idea of forever like it might bite me. My chest tightens every time the topic comes up. I keep telling myself I'll feel ready when the time is right, but the truth is, every time I try to picture myself walking down that aisle, I see nothing. Just white noise and a hollow ache where excitement should be. I've been dodging dates and venues and every conversation that starts with forever.

"You knew I needed time," I say.

"Yeah," he replies, voice tight. "I just didn't know it was time for someone else." He grabs his keys and leaves without slamming the door, but that makes it worse.

I clean the kitchen with shaking hands, and every wipe across the counter is too hard and fast. When the porch creaks, I'm not expecting anyone.

But Grayson is standing there, brow furrowed. He signs, ***"You okay?"***

I shake my head, eyes already burning. He steps inside without asking, without needing to. Just reaches for me, steady and sure. And I let myself fall apart in his arms.

We stand like that for a while. His arms around me. My forehead pressed to his chest. He doesn't ask questions. Just holds steady like he always did before everything went sideways.

Finally, I step back and wipe my face with the sleeve of my hoodie. ***"Sorry,"*** I sign, blinking fast. ***"You didn't come here for this."***

Grayson shakes his head. ***"I came to check the water lines. Saw his truck peel out."*** He pauses. ***"Figured something was wrong."***

"He thinks you're here too much."

Grayson doesn't flinch. Doesn't look away. ***"Am I?"***

I look at him, really look. The new lines around his eyes. The way he doesn't fill a room with noise but with presence. The steadiness he fought to earn. ***"No."***

He exhales slowly. ***"Then what's really wrong?"***

I shake my head. ***"I don't know. I thought I'd be ready by now. The wedding. A future. But something feels... stuck."***

Grayson studies me. ***"Because of me?"***

I look down at my hands, ***"Because of me. I don't know what I want anymore."***

He signs carefully. ***"You don't have to know yet. You just have to be honest about it."***

My eyes sting again. ***"It's not just about Teddy. It's about Clara. About what kind of life I'm building for her. About who I am now."***

Grayson nods. ***"Then start there."***

"And if I mess it up?"

He reaches out, gently brushing his fingers down my arm. ***"Then you start again."***

We don't say much after that. Grayson moves into the kitchen like he belongs there, fills the kettle without asking, and sets two mugs on the counter. I sit at the table, fingers curled around the hem of my sleeve, and watch him.

It's quiet. Easy. Familiar in a way that shouldn't feel this natural. He hands me a mug and leans back against the counter, sipping his own.

"Remember that diner outside Phoenix?" I sign. ***"The one with the jukebox that only played Patsy Cline?"***

He smiles. ***"You threatened to quit the tour if Jensen didn't take you somewhere else."***

"And you told the waitress I was a country star with stage fright." We both laugh; the kind that pulls a little ache with it.

I remember him crashing onto the hotel couch after a show, covered in sweat and glitter from Delilah's confetti cannon. I threw him a towel. He threw it back and said, ***"I don't need clean. I need coffee."***

Back then, everything was loud. Now... it's quiet. And somehow more intimate. The floorboards creak overhead.

Clara.

She comes down the stairs, rubbing her eyes, her hair wild from sleep. She stops when she sees Grayson and signs, ***"You're still here?"***

He nods. ***"Yeah. Just for a little while."***

She crosses the room, climbs onto his lap like it's second nature, and rests her head on his shoulder. I can't breathe for a second.

After she falls asleep again, Grayson stands and gently gathers her into his arms. Clara barely stirs, her cheek pressed to his shoulder, one hand still clutching her goat plushie. I follow him upstairs, trailing behind in silence.

He moves like he's done this a thousand times, like it's instinct. My throat tightens when he pulls back the covers and settles her into bed, tucking the blanket up to her chin. He brushes a curl off her forehead, and she sighs in her sleep.

My hands curl around the banister. I don't move. Just watch the way he balances strength with gentleness. The way Clara melts into him like she's always belonged there. My throat tightens so hard it feels like breathing is suddenly a luxury I can't afford.

For just a moment, I imagine a version of this life where we didn't fall apart, where tours ended, and home was something we built together instead of something we circled around and missed. It hurts how easily I can see it, how much it looks like peace.

And it hits me.

This is what it could have been. All along. Not perfect, not easy, but real.

A life we never let ourselves have.

He turns toward me, and I manage a smile I don't quite feel. When I return downstairs, Grayson is quietly rinsing out the mugs in the kitchen. The space feels warmer, as if his presence has settled into the air.

He glances at me, then signs, ***"You should get some sleep."***

I nod, moving to walk him to the door. We linger there, caught in a moment that stretches a little too long, not uncomfortable, just... weighted. ***"Want to come to the farmer's market this weekend?"*** I ask. ***"With us?"***

He nods. ***"Yeah. I'd like that."***

I close the door behind him and lean against it, the house's quiet settling around me. Later, I sit at the kitchen table with a pen and Clara's baby book. I flip to a blank page.

I don't know what I'll write yet.

But I'm ready to stop avoiding the blank spaces. Maybe it won't be perfect. Maybe it won't be anything like I imagined. But it'll be real. And that's enough to begin with.

Chapter 41

Grayson

I wake up before the sun. The apartment is still, the kind of stillness I never used to know how to sit in. Now, I let it settle over me like proof I survived something I wasn't sure I would. The coffee pot sputters. I lean against the counter and watch the steam rise, hands wrapped around a chipped mug Jude found at a thrift shop. It has a cartoon goat saying, "Mornings are baaad." He said it felt appropriate. I didn't argue.

After I finish my coffee, I feed the stray cat that decided my porch is hers. She's skittish, orange, and has a notch in one ear. I don't know her name, but she shows up like clockwork, so I show up too. It feels good to have something to take care of.

I pull on my boots and head out. There's fencing to check on the south side of Maddie's property, and I promised her dad I'd help finish the new coop by the end of the week.

I don't expect to see Teddy at the hardware store. But there he is, by the posthole diggers, jaw tight. He nods. I nod back.

He eyes the supplies in my arms. "You working full-time out there now?"

I sign slowly, evenly. ***"Just helping where I can."***

His eyes narrow. "Right."

I feel the old reflex that used to tighten my jaw and curl my fists, but it fades. These days, I save my fire for things that matter. I just keep walking. I didn't come here to fight. At the ranch, Maddie's dad is already out by the coop. I work quietly, matching his pace. He doesn't ask questions. Just hands me nails when I need them. Clara comes out after lunch with lemonade and sits in the grass, drawing the coop like a castle. She tells me it needs a flag on top. I promise to add one.

Later, after the sun dips behind the trees, my phone buzzes. It's a picture from Maddie. Clara, in new overalls, standing beside a goat on top of a hay bale.

Chaos legacy lives on, the caption reads.

My thumb hovers over the screen. Her smile. The hay. The goat trying to chew the string off her overalls. It's all joy. It's everything I never thought I'd get to witness. I don't realize I'm smiling until my eyes sting. Then I save it to my favorites.

That night, I sketch out plans for a wooden swing to hang from the tree near the chicken run. Just an idea. Something for Clara. A part of me still builds like I'm preparing to disappear.

Like nothing good lasts. But this time, I sketch slowly. Intentionally. I might actually get to watch her use it.

But I don't want to leave.

And I may not be afraid to admit it for the first time in a long time.

Clara's birthday is coming up. Six. How the hell did that happen? This year, Maddie let me help plan it. It's nothing huge, just close friends, animals, cake, and chaos. Clara wants pink balloons, a goat-shaped cake, and a scavenger hunt in the barn. I offer to build the signs for the hunt and paint them myself. She beams when I show her the sketches.

The morning of the party, I'm hanging the last streamers when Maddie walks up to me, phone in hand. ***"Your parents are on their way. And... your sisters too."***

I freeze. It's not that I didn't expect them, it's just that I never do. When they arrive, I see them from the kitchen window. My mom is the first out of the car, arms full of wrapped boxes. My dad moves slower, shoulders set, but there's something different about how he carries himself.

Then I see my sisters. Both of them. I haven't seen them in years. The backyard seems to still. Clara doesn't notice. She's too busy bouncing between gift bags and goats.

My mom hugs me. Her eyes are glassy. ***"You look good,"*** she signs, her hands smooth and practiced, familiar.

My sisters tentatively hug me, then immediately drop to the grass with Clara like it's the most natural thing in the world.

My dad doesn't say anything right away. He just stands a few feet off, hands in his jacket pockets and eyes on Clara.

Then, slowly, clumsily, he signs, ***"Happy birthday."*** It's not smooth. His fingers hesitate. But it's there. Real.

I stare at him. Then nod.

He tries again. ***"You... are a good..."*** He struggles. Frowns. Then just signs, ***"Son."***

The word stumbles out of his hands like it weighs something. *Son.* And for the first time in a long time, I believe it's meant for me, the real me and not the version he wanted. The one I am.

I don't know what to say. So I don't. I just stand there, trying to keep my chest from shaking. And he claps my shoulder like maybe he knows.

There's too much in my chest to name. Anger, I buried. Hope I tried to kill. And something new, something like healing, but too raw to say for sure. I watch him walk away toward the porch, where my mom and Maddie chat, their movements casual and happy. My sisters are still sprawled in the grass with Clara, sur-rounded by crayons, stickers, and the kind of joy I used to think belonged to other people.

I stay where I am, rooted to the spot.

Because my dad tried, he showed up, not just physically, but in a way that counts. How I spent years wishing he would and convincing myself I didn't need him to. My hands shake just a little. I tuck them into my pockets.

It's not forgiveness. Not yet. But it's something. A start. The smallest crack in a wall, I stopped believing would ever come down.

And when Clara runs toward me a minute later, goat plushie in one hand, birthday crown crooked on her head, and signs, ***"Did you see my cake?!"*** I catch her mid-jump and spin her once.

"Best cake I've ever seen," I sign back.

And everything feels almost right for the first time in a long time. Like I belong here. Like I might stay long enough to see the swing hung and for the word *son* to finally feel true.

Chapter 42
Maddie

The house is quiet again, lit only by the porch light and the soft hum of a warm evening settling in. I'm leaning against the railing, arms folded loosely across my chest, a half-empty glass of sweet tea beside me.

Grayson steps out of the shadows signing, ***"You okay?"***

I nod, but it's not convincing. Too slow. Too careful. ***It was a good day,"*** I sign back, ***"because of you."***

He shakes his head, ***"Because of her."***

I turn to face him. There's something raw inside me that's been building since the last guest left. I know he can see it. ***"No,"*** I sign. ***"Because you stayed."***

Everything shifts. "I don't know what I'm doing," I say out loud, barely more than a whisper. "Not with Teddy. Not with this. Not with how I feel."

Grayson steps closer.

"But when I saw you today with Clara, with your family, I felt it. That thing I thought I'd buried. The one that used to scare the hell out of me."

He signs, ***"What thing?"***

I lift my hands slowly. ***"Hope."***

Then I move. One step. Then another. Every step toward him feels like peeling back something I thought had scarred over. But he's standing there like he's never moved. Like he waited without expecting anything. And maybe that's why it feels safe to fall now.

My fingers find the collar of his shirt. His hands find my waist. There's no hesitation, just the crash of something inevitable. When I kiss him, it's wildfire. Hungry. Reckless. Like everything we've held back is finally breaking loose. He presses me back against the porch post, one hand in my hair, the other anchoring me like he's afraid I'll disappear. I slide my hands under his shirt. I don't want to stop.

I want to burn in this.

But then, I do. My breath hitches. My palms flatten against his chest.

I don't pull away because I don't want him. I pull away because wanting him scares me more than anything. Because if I keep going, there won't be anything left of me to offer Teddy. And that feels cruel. Even if it's true.

"Grayson." I don't say more, but I know he sees it in my eyes. Not regret, just fear. Realization, something breaking loose inside me that isn't ready yet.

He pulls back immediately and signs, *"Sorry."*

I shake my head. *"Don't be. It's just... a lot."*

He nods. *"Yeah."*

I slip inside the house before I lose my nerve. He doesn't follow. That night, I sleep in fits and starts. The sheets are cold. I sit at the edge of the bed before dawn, fingers tangled in Clara's baby blanket. I want to cry and scream and smile all at once. I kissed him. I almost didn't stop. And now... I don't know who I'm hurting more. Him. Teddy. Or myself.

The next morning, Teddy knocks before the sun is up. He looks tired. Hollow. "We need to talk," he says.

We step off the porch together. The air is cool, but not enough to chase the heat rising in my chest.

"I can't do this anymore," he says. "You have to choose. Me or him."

I freeze. "Teddy"

"You say you're not ready. That you need time. But he's always here. Fixing things. Playing family."

"Because he's Clara's father," I snap. "Because I can't, won't cut him out of her life."

"Even if it costs you us?"

I don't answer. Not fast enough.

"Who's been there for her, Maddie? When she had strep? When did she have her first dance recital? Who helped you pay for that damn therapy horse? It wasn't him."

My voice breaks. "It wasn't fair to ask him to be. He was sick. He was getting help."

"I know. But I can't keep standing here wondering when I'll stop being second place to someone who didn't even know she existed."

I cover my mouth with one hand. The tears fall before I can stop them.

"I love you," he says, quiet now. "But I can't do this anymore."

I nod. "I know."

He slips the ring from my finger. There's no drama. No raised voices. Just a final gentle hug. Then he walks to his truck. Gets in. Drives away.

I stay rooted, unable to move. I'm already crying, but it's like my body hasn't caught up. I just stand there, staring at the gravel, waiting for something, anything, to make it make sense. And

I stand in the driveway barefoot, the gravel biting at my soles, watching the dust settle behind him like the end of a chapter I don't know how to finish.

I come inside just as Clara is waking up. Her curls are tangled, and her goat plushie is clutched under one arm. She rubs her eyes and stares at the door like she's waiting.

"What's *wrong, Mommy?"* Clara signs looking up at me, her eyes still sleepy.

I kneel down in front of her, swallowing past the tightness in my throat. I sign slowly, carefully, ***"Teddy had to go home, sweetheart. You might not see him for a while."***

Clara's brows furrow. She looks confused, then hurt. Her lip wobbles. ***"But he was going to make pancakes."***

My heart twists.

"I know," I say softly, brushing her hair back. ***"I'm sorry, bug."***

She processes that. Nods. Then looks up again. ***"Does that mean Daddy will stay more now?"***

I freeze. She called him Daddy. My throat closes around the lump rising fast. I sign back, hands shaking slightly. ***"Would you like that?"***

Clara lights up. ***"Yes. He's fun. He always makes things for me. He listens, even when I don't sign fast."***

I press a hand to my chest. It hurts because I'm afraid I'll fall apart if I don't anchor myself. I don't say anything else. I just pull Clara into my arms and press a kiss on her curls. And I know, without saying it, that this messy, broken, beautiful new beginning is where everything shifts.

Later that morning, I send a text with trembling fingers:

Clara wants to know if you'll make pancakes.

It takes him three minutes to reply.

I'll be there in fifteen. I've... never made pancakes before.

I grin despite everything.

When he shows up, Clara is already bouncing at the kitchen table, her goat plushie buckled into a seat beside her. Grayson walks in, sleeves rolled up, eyes wide.

"Okay," I say, stepping back from the counter. ***"You're on, chef."***

He signs, ***"I Googled it. I got this."***

He does not have this. Fifteen minutes in, the kitchen smells vaguely of burnt batter and something unidentifiable. There's flour on the floor, batter on the cabinets, and a stubborn glob of egg stuck in Grayson's hair.

Clara is giggling so hard she can barely stay upright in her seat. She signs, ***"This is the best breakfast ever."***

Grayson mock-scowls at her, then signs, ***"You're fired from quality control."***

She signs back, ***"You're fired from pancakes."***

I'm laughing now, real and full and messy. Somehow, amidst the chaos, he manages one decent pancake. A little misshapen, a little overcooked, but Clara claps like he just won a gold medal.

And when he slides it onto her plate with a sheepish smile, I feel something settle inside me.

It's not perfect, but life rarely is.

Chapter 43

Grayson

The scent of syrup and burnt batter still clings to my shirt. Clara's movements shake the pillows and send a grin across her face, pure energy and joy. Maddie folds laundry nearby, hair twisted in a loose knot, her calm steady in a way I don't think I've ever really known. I sip my coffee, leaning against the kitchen doorway. I'm not sure what this is supposed to feel like, being a father, being here, but this, right now, feels like something real. Not the mess of before. Not the ache of what I lost. Just... this.

Six months ago, I woke up in a halfway house with more guilt than clarity. Now, I get early morning texts from Maddie asking if I want to make pancakes for Clara. I'd never made them before, but I tried. I try everything.

And somehow, I haven't ruined it yet.

Outside, I haul my tool bag into the back of the truck, ready to tackle the nesting boxes Maddie's dad kept saying they didn't need until Clara insisted her chickens deserved "deluxe suites." I'm latching the tailgate when tires crunch across the gravel.

A dark SUV pulls up. I squint. I know that car. It's the same one the label used to give us when we were in town.

Delilah steps out first, her curls tucked under a wide-brimmed hat. She's wearing oversized sunglasses like armor. Alexander's right behind her, tall and tense, phone in hand. And behind them, Jensen and Lily.

I don't move. For a moment, I don't even breathe.

Delilah lowers her sunglasses slowly. ***"Hey, Gray."*** She is way too casual. Like this is a coffee shop. Like it hasn't been years.

I lift my hands. ***"What are you doing here?"***

Alexander gives a slight smile. ***"We were headed toward Austin. Jensen said you were here. So we decided to stop by instead of going to the airport, figured you wouldn't mind."***

Jensen raises his hand in a silent apology. ***"I didn't think we'd just show up. They kind of overruled me."***

Lily nudges him. ***"We've wanted to see you. All of us."***

I swallow. My palms itch. ***"It's been a long time."***

"Too long," Delilah says, stepping closer. ***"You look good, Gray. Really good."***

I nod. I don't know what to say to that. She used to see me at my worst. She peeled me off the bathroom floor more than once.

Now she's here, trying not to look like she's holding her breath.

"I'm sober. Working. Living here."

Alexander's eyebrows lift slightly. *"Seriously? You're living in a town with chickens, goats, and no sound check?"*

I smirk. *"I like the peace."*

Delilah smiles, but it falters as her gaze drifts toward the house. *"So, Clara's here? You're... really part of her life?"*

I nod, slower this time. *"Yeah. She calls me Daddy now."*

The moment stretches. It's not awkward, just heavy.

"Is she okay with us being here?" Lily asks. *"We don't want to overwhelm her."*

"She's never met a stranger and I think she'd like to meet you. She's got my eyes."

There's a long beat. Then the front door opens. Maddie steps out onto the porch, squinting into the sun. Clara peeks out behind her, then gasps when she sees that someone is with me.

"Daddy! You have friends! Hello friends!" She races toward me. I catch her and swing her into my arms. Her small hands press against my cheeks, signing quickly. *"Daddy, why are all these people staring at us?"*

I laugh, signing back. *"They're friends from before you were born. Want to meet them?"*

She tilts her head, then gives a solemn nod. Maddie walks over slowly, shoulders tight, gaze sweeping across the group. "Well," she says. "Didn't expect this today."

"No one ever does with us," Delilah replies gently. ***"Hi, Clara. I'm Delilah."***

Clara nods, polite but cautious. Alexander signs, ***"And I'm Alexander."***

"And I'm Lily. I am so excited to meet you. You know my daughter Lorelei is about your age. Maybe y'all can have a play date one day."

Clara eyes them all curiously. ***"They talk a lot,"*** she signs.

I grin. ***"Yeah. But they're nice."***

We sit outside under the shade tree near the garden. Delilah offers Clara a small keychain with a cartoon drum set. Clara lights up. Alexander tries to teach her a handshake. Jensen keeps glancing at me like he still doesn't believe I'm here. That I'm okay. Then, as the sun stretches across the grass, something takes the breath out of me. My dad pulls into the driveway. I forgot he asked to stop by. He climbs out of the truck, holding a bag of tools, and stops cold when he sees the group gathered.

Clara jumps down and signs rapidly. ***"Grandpa!"***

He signs back. ***"Hey, bunny."***

There's a beat of stunned silence. I knew my parents were coming to town soon. I didn't realize they were already here.

Delilah's eyes widen. *"He signs?"*

My dad shrugs, walking over. *"I've been taking lessons. I figured I should be able to talk to my granddaughter...to my son."*

It's still clumsy. Slow. But it's more than I ever expected. Clara beams and grabs his hand, pulling him toward the garden.

Delilah leans close, signing, *"Okay, maybe the boonies have changed you."*

"Not changed," I respond. *"Just... finally becoming who I wanted to be."*

Chapter 44

Maddie

The kitchen buzzes with morning energy, alive with the rhythm of the family routine. Dad sits at the worn wooden table, signing as he talks, while my three brothers chatter back and forth in a blend of speech and quick, effortless signs. The clatter of plates and the hiss of the coffee pot blend with the smell of bacon sizzling on the stove and eggs frying, a warm, familiar scent that settles deep in my chest.

Sunlight spills through the dusty windowpanes, casting long, golden bars across the floorboards, dust motes dancing lazily in the beams. The old wooden table creaks under the weight of heavy plates heaped with eggs, bacon, and thick slices of toast.

Clara weaves between legs, her bright eyes shining as she signs to her toy goat, telling it a story with confident, quick fingers. Her fingers paint an imaginary battle between her goat and an unseen dragon. She pauses, looking up at me with a grin full of excitement, her eyes sparkling with the thrill of the tale.

Mom moves with purpose, packing coolers with sandwiches, fresh fruit, and thermoses of coffee for the cattle drive. The soft scrape of lids and zip of coolers closing punctuate the morning bustle. Her face is calm but focused, shoulders squared with the weight of this trip.

Dad glances out the window and signs, ***"The creek's low this year, but the pasture's green. It'll be a long haul to the summer range, at least two weeks if we take the horses and keep to the old routes."***

One of my brothers grins and nudges me playfully. ***"You won't be missing your phone out there, since you're staying behind."***

I smile, signing back, ***"Good. I'd miss having it close."*** The thought brings a small comfort being here, steady, with Grayson and Clara holding the fort in a way.

Clara settles nearby, signing excitedly about her goat's latest adventure, her fingers effortlessly flying over the air. I smile back and sign, ***"Sounds like you've got your hands full."*** She repeatedly lifts her toy goat into the air, miming the imaginary fight with grand, sweeping gestures.

The front door creaks, and Grayson steps inside, his eyes wide as he takes in the bustle. He catches my glance and signs, ***"What's going on?"*** His presence steadies me, a quiet strength that's become our foundation.

I smile and say, ***"We're moving the herd to a new pasture. It's the big trip of the year."***

He nods and steps further in. ***"Want me to stay here? Keep the ranch running?"***

Mom looks up from the cooler and signs warmly, ***"I'm going to visit my sister in Willow Creek. Haven't seen her in a year."***

I squeeze Grayson's hand. ***"We'll hold down the ranch while they're gone. It's a good plan."*** The weight of responsibility feels lighter knowing he's here.

His quiet confidence steadies me. ***"I'll keep things steady here."***

Outside, the men saddle up, horses stamping softly on the dry dirt. Their movements are familiar and steady, the rhythm of a tradition carried through generations. I watch them ride into the morning before loading Clara into the truck.

After Clara's off to school, I saddle my horse and turn toward the far edge of the property. The leather creaks softly beneath my hands as I tighten the cinch, the sun climbing higher and heat rippling off the dusty dirt and sagebrush.

"Fence checking's the big job this time of year," I say, signing along with my words to Grayson. ***"I'll start at the far side. You start near the house and work your way out."***

He nods eagerly.

The ranch stretches wide beneath the blazing sun, every inch soaked with dust and history. I slide my fingers over the rough wire, feeling its stubborn resistance. A loose post sways faintly; I step down, pressing my heel into the dry dirt to steady it.

The sharp and grounding scent of sage fills my lungs, mixed with the faint sweetness of wildflowers clinging stubbornly to life on the dry earth. My horse shifts next to me, patient and steady, with a quiet rhythm to this endless work.

As I hammer the post, my mind drifts to Grayson, how far he's come since those dark days when addiction nearly broke him. Eighteen months in rehab, three more in a halfway house, and just four months out, fighting every day to stay sober. He didn't know about Clara until recently, a secret I carried alone for so long. Now, faced with this unexpected fatherhood, he's stepping up in ways I never dared hope for. He's no longer the broken man who left us wondering if he'd ever be whole again. Now, he's carving out a new life here on the ranch, steady and sure, like the earth beneath my feet. After almost ten years of loving him through all the disappointments and the distance, it finally feels like I have a partner I can count on in this hard life.

I glance over the horizon, the blue sky stretching endlessly above, and think about Clara —her bright mind, quick fingers, and how she brings light into every corner of this place. It's hard, messy, and perfect to raise her here with Grayson by my side. Mounting back up, I head to my next checkpoint.

Lost in thought, I don't see the ground gopher hole until my horse's foot falls right in it. There's a sudden, sickening crunch. The horse stumbles violently, panic flooding its eyes. "Whoa! Easy, easy!" I shout, trying to calm it, but my boot catches in the stirrup.

The animal bucks hard, throwing me forward against the saddle horn. Pain explodes in my ribs and arm. Then the sickening snap, the horse's leg collapses beneath it. The animal whinnies in terror, thrashing wildly.

One flailing hoof pins me down, hammering into my side.

Fire blooms across my ribs. I gasp, trying to shield myself, but the weight and movement crush me. My head spins, the world tilting wildly. The horse's panic thrashes around me, deafening and violent. Each wild kick hammers the ground and me, the force jarring through my bones and shaking every nerve.

My vision swims and blurs. Breathing sharpens into ragged gasps. Pain slices through my chest and ribs, fierce and relentless. Desperate, I reach for my phone, not in my saddlebag, but in the pocket of my riding jacket. My fingers tremble as I fumble to pull it free, every movement slow and clumsy through the haze of pain and panic.

I press it tight against my chest, heart pounding fiercely in my ears, willing Grayson to feel the faint buzz, the lifeline vibrating through the space between us and into his pocket. I imagine him nearby, his phone nestled against his body, the vibration rippling through the fabric like a silent alarm.

My breath catches, shallow and ragged. Each inhale is a sharp stab in my ribs. The world tilts; sounds and colors blur and distort at the edges of my vision. With trembling hands, I unlock the screen, my eyes fluttering as the pain steals my focus. I dial his number, listening to the endless ring that feels like it stretches into forever.

No answer.

Time drags. My chest tightens, panic clawing its way up. Fighting the darkness creeping in, I tap out one last desperate message, my fingers barely able to steady themselves.

911

The text sends a fragile hope flickering in the cold void. Then the world slips away beneath me and darkness pulls me under.

Darkness wraps around me like a thick fog, soft but endless. I'm slipping, floating somewhere between here and nowhere. Shapes blur above me, faces half-seen, edged with light and shadow. Their voices sound distant, as if through a heavy curtain. Someone's hand brushes my cheek, calm and steady. The touch is gentle and careful, but urgency pulses beneath it. I try to open my eyes, but they feel swollen and heavy, like lead curtains. Blinking is like swimming through molasses.

A sharp scent slices through the haze, antiseptic, cold, clinical. So different from the earth and sage of the ranch. It makes my stomach lurch. Somewhere nearby, a stretcher clicks into place. Boots crunch against gravel. The murmur of voices floats in and out, calm but clipped. There's wind now, strong and uneven, and the rhythmic *whop-whop-whop* of helicopter rotors overhead.

Flashes of red and blue streak across my closed eyelids. The light pulses against my skin. I can't tell if I'm dreaming or drowning in it.

Then the world shifts.

Hands grip the edges of my stretcher. I'm lifted off the ground, wind roaring around me, the dry bite of dust in my mouth. The rotors get louder, stronger, until their vibration rumbles through my chest. I'm carried toward the open belly of the helicopter, then loaded inside with practiced precision. The interior lights are stark, the beeping steady. As we rise, I catch a glimpse through the open side door, patchwork fields shrinking fast, the ranch vanishing beneath us.

Home fading into the distance.

The relentless vibration shakes through my body, every bump and turn sending jolts through my aching ribs and shattered bones. Fluorescent lights buzz overhead, relentless and stark. I taste the sterile coldness of the recycled air mixed with the faint metallic tang of blood and medicine. My breath comes in shallow, uneven gasps, each inhale stabbing sharp through my chest.

I want to call out to say something, but my voice is gone, swallowed by the weight pressing down on my broken body. Memories flicker like broken film:

Grayson's hand, steady and warm, squeezing mine.

The way his lips felt pressed softly against mine.

Clara's bright eyes lighting up when she learns a new sign, her fingers dancing with joy.

The first time Grayson held Clara, both silent and perfect.

Hold on, Maddie.

I want to believe it. I have to. A nurse's hand brushes my hair back, warm against my skin.

"We have you," she says gently. "Hold on. Stay with us."

My eyelids flutter, heavy but unwilling to close. Somewhere, distant but clear, I hear the faint beeping of machines, steady and familiar. Just hold on. The world sways, blinks, then fades again.

Chapter 45

Grayson

I crouch by the fence post, the sun blazing, sweat tracing hot trails beneath my shirt. My phone vibrates against my leg, a faint but steady shake catches my eye through the sleeve of my jacket. I pull it out, heart skipping when the screen lights up. One missed call from Maddie.

A lump forms in my throat. My fingers tremble as I type a desperate message.

Me: *Maddie? Where are you? What's wrong?*

Seconds stretch into a maddening silence. No reply. No comfort. I switch to FaceTime, hoping to catch her face, any sign of where she is or what's wrong. The screen blinks, but no one answers. That moment is the worst, an empty space where hope slips away. My chest tightens until it feels like my ribs will crack.

I send a quick text to Jude with shaking hands.

Me: *Maddie's hurt. No idea where. Need help now.*

His reply comes almost instantly.

Jude: *Calm down. Where did she say she was headed?*

I replay everything I know from that morning.

Me: *She went out to check the fence on the far pasture, while I was closer to the house.*

Jude: *Okay. Stay put. I'm coming with someone.*

The dull roar of helicopter blades rumbles overhead, vibrating through my bones like a warning. I look up just in time to see the chopper cutting a silver arc across the sky, heading straight for the ranch.

Another message comes from Jude.

Jude: *Search and rescue is on it. Keep your phone near.*

Without thinking, I drop the post and run toward the house, adrenaline flooding my limbs even as my mind spins. Time slows to a crawl. I stare at my phone, willing it to light up with more news. Then comes the message that strikes me cold.

Jude: *Found her. Badly injured. The horse was put down. Life flight to the hospital. Hold for more info.*

My breath catches. My throat closes. I want to scream, but nothing comes out. Clara is finishing school soon, so I need to be with her. I suck in a deep, ragged breath and shove the panic down deeper than I ever thought possible. I have to be strong.

Clara's face lights up when she spots me waiting outside her school. She runs forward, wrapping her arms tightly around my waist, and for a moment, all the fear and chaos fade, replaced by her warmth, her light.

I sign softly, ***"Hey, bug."*** She doesn't ask about Mom yet. Instead, she grins and lifts her backpack proudly.

"School was good." Her innocence is both a blessing and a weight. For now, that normal moment is all I need to hold onto.

The drive home is heavy with silence, the sun slipping low and shadows stretching long across the dusty ranch road. Clara's fingers trace lazy patterns on the window glass, signing softly to herself, a small comfort against the storm swirling inside me.

When we pull into the driveway, Jude's truck is there. Jude steps out, sharp and precise in his tailored suit, starkly contrasting with the warm, casual woman beside him. ***"This is Martha,"*** Jude says, motioning her forward. ***"She'll stay with Clara while you come with me. She's great with kids."*** Clara studies Martha carefully but doesn't protest.

I kneel to Clara's level, signing gently. ***"Martha's going to keep you company, but I need to go with Jude for a while."*** Her fingers tremble for a moment before she signs back, ***"Okay."***

I squeeze her hand, adding, ***"Everything's going to be fine."***

Martha smiles warmly, and I see Clara relax just a fraction. Jude claps me on the shoulder.

"Keep it together, Gray. For Maddie. For Clara."

I nod, gripping the door handle until my knuckles go white. The ride to the hospital is a blur—a mix of fear twisting deep in my gut and a thousand swirling thoughts. The world around me feels muted and dull. I feel like I'm watching everything from underwater. Every possible nightmare flashes behind my eyes. But Jude is steady beside me, a calm anchor in the chaos.

"You can't lose it now," he signs.

I close my eyes, forcing slow, steady breaths.

For Maddie. For Clara.

The hospital lights stab at my senses as we walk inside. Cold and clinical, the antiseptic smell hits me hard, so different from the dusty warmth of the ranch. Jude clasps my arm.

"Stay with me," he tells me. *"I'm getting you in."*

Inside, the quiet hum of fluorescent lights buzzes overhead. Nurses and doctors bustle past, faces blurred in my panic. At reception, Jude doesn't hesitate.

"He's her husband," he tells the nurse. *"We need to see Maddie. Now."* The weight of the word *husband* hits me hard, years of mistakes and silence crashing in. If we make it through this, I promise myself I'm marrying her. Like I should have years ago.

Jude glances at me, reading the fire burning in my eyes. *"You're holding it together fine. Keep holding on."*

Seconds later, a doctor leads us down a narrow corridor with blinking machines and cold steel. In the room, Maddie lies pale and fragile, tubes snaking from her body, monitors blinking steadily.

Her chest rises and falls slowly and steadily. I reach for her hand, trembling, brushing my fingers against her cool skin. She opens her eyes, foggy but aware, and squeezes my hand weakly.

I sign, ***"Hey."***

Her eyes flicker to me, a faint smile tugging at her lips.

I lean closer and mouth, *I'm here. We're going to get through this.* Her grip tightens just a little. I wipe a stray tear, the weight of everything crashing down. Years of regret, hope, and love converge in that moment. And I know this is just the beginning.

Jude lowers his hands and begins signing slowly, carefully, his face grave but steady. ***"She's in serious condition,"*** he says. ***"Serious... but stable."***

I nod, barely breathing. *Stable* is a fragile word to cling to.

Jude's fingers move again. ***"Pelvis crushed. Broken leg."*** He pauses, then adds, ***"Ribs fractured. Head injury."***

The weight slams into me. My vision blurs momentarily, but Jude's calm, deliberate signs hold me steady.

"Luckily, they found her fast," he signs next. ***"Early treatment is critical."*** I clench my jaw, nodding though the ache inside won't lessen.

His hand pats my arm before he continues. ***"You're doing good. Stay strong."***

I swallow, fire burning in my chest. For Maddie and Clara, I have to hold it together.

Chapter 46

Maddie

I lie back against the stiff hospital mattress, the antiseptic sting in the air scraping the back of my throat. It's sharp, clinical, so different from the dusty warmth of the ranch I'm used to. Tubes snake in and out of me like alien vines, and machines beep in a steady, relentless rhythm that echoes in my ears like a mechanical heartbeat I can't escape.

The light above is harsh, too bright for my swollen, heavy eyes. I blink slowly, trying to clear the fog clouding my brain. The pounding in my head is relentless, like a drum missing its rhythm, just noise, chaotic and unyielding. I'm not sure where my body ends and the pain begins. My pelvis throbs, sharp jabs slice through my ribs with every breath, and my leg feels shattered, aflame beneath the plaster cast.

I want to move, to grab something real, something mine, but my fingers twitch involuntarily, barely responding. The thin, plastic sheets beneath me crinkle with every shallow breath, and the cold, sterile chill of the room wraps around me like an icy blanket despite the sunlight pouring through the cracked blinds.

Then Grayson's hand finds mine, warm, steady, familiar. His fingers curl around mine with gentle certainty, pulling me back from the edge of the haze. I try to speak, but words feel like molasses in my mouth, slow and heavy. So I sign instead, clumsily, but with everything I have, ***"I'm here."***

He leans closer and signs back, ***"We're going to get through this."***

Hope flickers, a fragile candle fighting a brutal windstorm. But it's there.

The nurses come and go, voices gentle but brisk. They adjust my machines, check my vitals, and speak softly about healing and recovery. Their words blur, swallowed by pain and fatigue into meaningless noise. I want to understand, to grasp every word, but it feels impossible.

Flashbacks crash through the haze: Grayson's panicked face when he arrived, his signing by my bedside, and Clara's bright smile that morning before everything changed.

Fear coils deep, a serpent swallowing my courage. I wonder if I'm breaking beyond repair, if the strength I clung to for so long is cracking. But then Clara's face flashes in my mind, the light in her eyes, her small hands telling stories in signs, and suddenly, the fight surges back, fierce and relentless.

Guilt gnaws, too, over moments I've already lost, the silence Grayson shoulders alone, and the chaos I brought crashing into this fragile family. But I push it aside, forcing myself to breathe, to hope, to fight. Because giving up isn't an option.

A steady pressure on my arm breaks through the swirl, then Jude's voice, calm but serious.

"They got to you just in time, Maddie. It could've been much worse."

I nod weakly, swallowing back tears that sting my eyes.

"Your injuries are severe. Broken bones. You've got a long road ahead."

I squeeze his hand, a silent promise that I will fight.

The hours stretch, long and slow. I drift between pain and sleep, caught in a haze of fractured dreams and distant, muffled sounds.

Sometimes, I wake up to see Grayson sitting beside me, signing words only for me, ***"Stay strong. I'm here."***

I cling to those words like a lifeline.

This broken body is mine to heal. This fractured family is mine to save.

And I will.

One afternoon, Jude sits quietly by my bed after a visit from Clara and Grayson. He looks at me and says softly, "Your Mom's been called. She's on her way home."

I blink, hope stirring inside me despite the ache. "I'll be glad to see her, but she'll probably hover." The thought of Clara back home feels like a thread pulling me toward something better, even if I'm scared of what it means.

Days pass in a fog. The physical pain is a constant, raw ache beneath every thought. I'm learning to breathe through it, to trust the slow, torturous work of healing.

The physical therapist arrives with a calm smile and steady hands. She moves me gently, coaxing muscles to respond where pain screams in protest. Every tiny twitch feels like a victory and a defeat all at once. I grit my teeth as waves of fire radiate through my ribs and pelvis while I try to shift just an inch.

"Small steps," she says, voice soft and patient. But all I feel is the crawl of time, the endless crawl toward recovery that feels like a lifetime.

Grayson visits every day. His presence steadies me. His hands tell the words I can't find. He never pushes and never asks too much. He just is my steady anchor in the storm.

Clara comes too, a burst of light in the hospital's dull world. Her fingers dance through the air, signing stories about goats, new games at school, little victories, and mischief. She never asks about the pain or the machines. She just holds my hand, a quiet reminder of why I fight.

Jude's visits tether me to reality. Calm and direct, he signs with Grayson, making sure both of them stay grounded. I watch their conversations, the way Jude holds space for us, a silent strength that keeps me from falling apart.

The doctors tell me the fractures are severe. Months, maybe a year on the outside time frame, before I can walk properly again. Pelvis, ribs, and leg each demanding time, care, and patience. Words I hate but must accept.

But I'm here. Fighting. Every twitch, every flutter of pain is proof I'm alive, still clawing my way home.

For the first time in years, hope feels like more than a flicker. It feels real.

With Grayson by my side and Clara waiting, I know I will get there.

Some nights, the pain dulls but the fear doesn't. I wake gasping, the accident replaying in my mind's eye: the snap, the panic in the horse's eyes, the swallowing darkness. My body shakes despite exhaustion. I clench my fists, trying to steady the storm inside.

A soft knock pulls my attention and then Grayson's fingers brush mine.

"You're safe," his hands promise. ***"I'm here."***

I hold onto that promise as the night closes back in.

Chapter 47

Grayson

The ranch feels off without Maddie. The usual rhythm, the soft signing drifting from the porch, Clara's quick fingers fluttering through the air, is stretched thin like a fragile thread ready to snap. The sun scorches the cracked dirt, casting long shadows over the fence posts, but it all settles heavy around me, dull and aching.

Clara and I try to build a new routine, but it's delicate and unstable. Her smiles don't come easy anymore. They're slower, weighted. Her hands sometimes tremble when she signs, like the absence of Maddie is an invisible weight crushing her petite frame. I catch her staring at the driveway too many times, as if watching for Maddie and willing her to appear.

I want to tell her it'll be okay, but the words won't come. Instead, I squeeze her hand, my fingers curling around hers before signing, ***"We're here. We're together."***

Her fingers tremble while she responds, ***"I miss her."***

The silence between us is thick, full of things too big for six-year-old shoulders and too raw for me to voice. It wraps tight around my ribs, squeezing, reminding me how fragile everything is.

Some nights, fear crashes over me like storm waves, wild and relentless. Maddie's injuries, the endless hospital days, and the slow, torturous road ahead all press down. Beneath it all, the dark whisper of old demons, relapse, failure, and losing everything lurks just beneath the surface.

I press my hands to my face, breath hitching. Then I sign, slow and steady, ***"I'm fighting. For you. For Mom. For us."***

She leans in, hand tightening around mine. At this moment, I'm not the broken addict I was. I'm a father, a protector, a promise.

Days bleed into one another: feeding goats in the dawn's chill, fixing fences under the unforgiving sun, helping Clara wrestle through schoolwork she sometimes finds too hard without Mom's gentle guidance. Every glance we share, every small joke we sign in the quiet, every little win feels like a thread weaving us closer. But the worry never leaves. The fear that this fragile new life could unravel haunts me, an ever-present shadow.

I find myself staring at the empty fields, picturing Maddie there, her hands shaping the air, her smile lighting the morning, and fighting the pull to fall back into the dark places I fought so hard to leave behind.

Instead, I focus on Clara's bright eyes, the way her fingers fly when she tells stories about the goats or games she plays with Martha, the caregiver who's become her constant when I'm working late or at the hospital. Clara is my anchor. The reason I keep going.

When the panic swells, when the weight of it all threatens to break me, I remind myself: *I'm here. I'm staying. We'll make it.*

The door swings open. Maddie's wheelchair rolls across the floorboards, the rumble oddly comforting now. Her eyes are tired but steady, surveying the living room, the home we're all fighting to hold together.

Clara sits cross-legged on the rug, drawing. Her fingers dance as she signs stories to her toy goat. When Maddie enters, her eyes lift and meet ours, warm and full of something I can't quite name, maybe relief, maybe hope.

Clara signs, ***"Mom, therapy today?"***

Maddie nods, her hand shaky but sure as she signs back. *"Harder than yesterday, but I'm getting stronger. Every day, a little better."*

Clara's brow furrows, lip trembling. She signs, *"I missed you so much. The hospital was cold and scary."*

Maddie pulls her into a gentle hug. Her fingers tremble, but her hold is firm. *"I missed you too, bug. Being away was the hardest thing. But I'm here now."*

I move closer and rest a hand on Maddie's knee. The pain must be constant, but she hides it well. The bruises and bandages still peek from beneath her hospital gown. She hates them but it makes changing the bandages easier; a fact she hated to admit when she was released.

Clara signs softly, *"Sometimes I'm scared. What if you have to go back?"*

Maddie's eyes glisten with tears, her hands signing with quiet conviction, *"I won't leave again. I promise. We'll take it one day at a time."*

I sign slowly, *"You're not alone. We're here. All of us."*

Later, evening settles. I help Maddie with the small, hard things she can't do alone. I ease her from the wheelchair to the bed, slowly and carefully. I tuck the blanket over her legs, feeling her wince but seeing the grateful smile she tries to hide.

She signs, *"Can you help me with my pajamas?"*

I nod and sit beside her, rolling the pajama pants up her legs step by step. Every move is careful, the pain sharp beneath the skin where bruises throb and bones ache.

Clara watches from the doorway, hands folded quietly. I catch her eye and smile. She signs, *"I want to help too."*

I nod back. *"We all help each other."*

After tucking Maddie in, I sit with Clara a while longer. We trace stories in the air, letting the day's weight settle. She's more sedate than usual, the weight of all this too much for her six years.

When I glance back at Maddie, she's asleep, her chest rising and falling slowly and steadily. I brush a stray curl from her forehead.

This isn't the life I imagined. It's harder, messier, rawer. But it's ours.

And somehow, that makes it worth fighting for.

The morning is brutal.

I haul water buckets, feed goats, and fix fences under the hot sun. Every step is heavy. Every breath labored. My muscles ache from days of little rest, but I push on. Maddie's watching from the porch, her face pale but determined.

Clara follows close behind, her small legs working hard, but her spirit dimmer than before.

The simplest tasks become mountains.

At one point, a post breaks loose. I kneel to fix it, sweat stinging my eyes. Clara watches, biting her lip, hesitant to sign, afraid to ask if Mom is going to be okay.

I want to promise her everything will be fine, but my heart races and the old fear gnaws in the back of my mind, what if I fail them? What if this all falls apart?

I swallow it down and force a smile, signing a silly joke to Clara. She laughs, the first authentic emotion from her in days, and it lights a small spark inside me.

But as the sun beats down, exhaustion seeps into my bones. I know Maddie's fight is just beginning, and so is ours.

We're treading water in a storm, but I swear, I'll keep us afloat.

The evening drags on slowly. Maddie's pain makes everything harder; moving, breathing, and even sitting up feels like a battle she's losing. I watch her wrestle with frustration, the pain sharpening her words and her temper. She snaps at me more than usual, and I get it. I'm exhausted too, worn thin from trying to be everything she needs.

When it's time to get ready for bed, I help her with the small tasks she can't manage alone. I notice the way she winces when I pull the pajama sleeves over her bruised arms, the soft curses she mutters under her breath when something hurts too much.

She's cranky, exhausted, and fed up with this broken body that won't cooperate.

I sit on the edge of the bed, watching her struggle with the blanket, her face tight with pain and frustration. I'm ready to say something, anything, but then she looks at me, eyes blazing, and lashes out again.

"Why do you have to stay so close all the time? You need sleep too," she signs sharply.

I don't hold back. I sign back quickly, ***"Why wouldn't I stay close to the woman I love, who needs me every damn night?"***

Her eyes widen, the shock hitting harder than any slap. In all the years we've been together and apart, getting those words from me is like a crack in a wall she thought was unbreakable.

She blinks, signs trembling but urgent, ***"You... love me?"***

I nod, my throat tight, signing slowly and surely, ***"Every day. Every minute."***

The weight of years of lost chances, broken promises, pain, and healing hangs heavy in the air between us. But in that moment, it's all real, all true.

She reaches out, trembling, and pulls me into a shaky embrace. I hold her like I never want to let go.

"Finally," she signs softly against my shoulder.

"Finally," I sign back, letting the words wash over us both, a balm for the long road ahead.

We settle beneath the blankets, close enough that even the cold can't touch us. Tonight, at least, we fight the dark together.

Chapter 48
Maddie

I steady myself against the worn armrest of the couch, the walker resting just a few feet away; my lifeline that feels both close and impossibly distant. My legs ache fiercely after this morning's therapy session. Every step was a battle, muscles screaming, tendons tight like steel cables stretched too far. My pelvis throbs as if bruised from every angle, and each shallow breath sends sharp jabs through my ribs. The pain is relentless, a heavy weight draped over me like a second skin.

The physical therapist tells me it's progress. Slow, frustrating progress. But all I see is how far I still have to go. The stairs, standing, walking without wincing, they're mountains I climb every day. The exhaustion drapes over me, heavier than my body.

Grayson sits nearby at the kitchen table, methodically sorting mail and bills. His fingers dance softly through the air as he signs quietly to himself, a habit when he's thinking. I watch the way his eyes flicker to me every so often, full of quiet concern and steady presence. His calm is a balm on the chaos inside my head but also a sharp reminder of how much everything has shifted.

I swallow hard, get his attention, and then sign slowly and deliberately, testing the words I've never voiced before. *"Grayson... can I ask you something?"* My fingers tremble, betraying the knot tightening in my chest.

His eyes lock on mine with the focus that always makes me feel seen. His hands hover, ready. *"Anything,"* he signs, steady as ever.

I close my eyes, gathering courage. The truth feels heavier than I imagined. *"About rehab... what was it really like for you?"* I ask, the words flowing easier once I start.

His face shifts. The calm darkens with old shadows. He signs slowly, deliberately, as if reliving every moment. *"Dark. Lonely. Every day, a fight. Fighting to breathe. Fighting the pull to give up."*

His hands tremble slightly, a rare crack in his otherwise steady facade. The room feels too quiet for a heartbeat, filled only with the weight of his truth. I bite my lip, tears slipping free. *"I'm sorry, Grayson,"* I sign, sadness and tenderness mingling in my chest.

He shrugs with a small, rueful smile as if he's carried that burden alone so long he doesn't know how to let it go. *"I fought because of you. Because I wanted to be better."*

I reach out and squeeze his hand, trembling with the effort. The tears come harder now, warm and genuine. He leans in, his lips brushing mine in a slow, tender kiss, the kind waiting beneath years of silence and regret.

The heat surges between us, wild, urgent, but I pull back, breath shaky. I sign, *"Not yet... my body..."* gesturing to the braces and scars that cage me, reminding me how fragile I remain.

He nods, understanding without question. His forehead presses softly to mine. *"Soon. I'll wait."*

For a moment, we hold each other silent but connected, two souls tangled in pain, hope, and love. I rest my head on his shoulder, inhaling the familiar scent of his shampoo and the faint trace of leather from his jacket. The house hums softly, the ticking clock, the distant fridge, a quiet cocoon. The weight of all we've survived presses in, but so does the promise of what's still possible.

When I finally pull away, I sign, *"I'm scared."*

He wraps his arms tighter, fingers brushing over mine, signing back, *"Me too. But not alone. We're in this together."*

That truth is a lifeline, anchoring me against fear.

I sit on the porch, the sun beating down hard and warm on my skin. My body aches deep inside from hours of therapy and restless nights. All I can do right now is PT, physical therapy that drains me completely, but is the only thing helping me inch forward. The walker sits close by, a constant reminder of how much I still can't do.

Grayson works out in the yard, hauling water buckets and fixing fence posts. I watch the sweat trace trails down his strong arms, the determined set of his jaw. His quiet strength steadies me in ways words never could. Clara trails behind him, her small legs moving fast to keep up. Her usual sparkle is back, brighter than I feel, as if she knows we're going to be okay because she's with us at home.

Grayson helps me dress, steadying me as I try to rise from the bed. Each movement sends sharp jabs through my ribs and pelvis, but his hands are calm and patient, a steady anchor. The physical therapist smiles warmly and guides me gently through exercises. Every slight twitch of muscle is a victory, even as pain screams beneath the surface.

Clara waits nearby with Martha, signing about new games and the goats. Their laughter bubbles up, a bright spot in the fog clouding my mind. Grayson carries me back after therapy, quiet and strong, my unexpected hero. I remember Grayson holding my hand on the first day of rehab, tentative but full of promise. Hope felt distant then. Now, fragile but real hope lives here in this house.

Grayson reads stories to Clara, his fingers tracing the air and painting pictures with signs.

I rest, exhausted but alive. The road ahead is long and steep. But we walk it together.

Chapter 49

Grayson

The ranch hums with life again.

It's been months since the accident, and Maddie is walking more confidently every day, even if she still tires faster than she wants to admit. She's stubborn as hell. Refuses help half the time. But I stay close anyway. I've learned that love isn't about grand gestures. Sometimes it's quiet. Bringing her the walker before she asks. Holding her elbow when she pretends she doesn't need it. Rubbing the stiffness from her back when she falls asleep on the couch with her book open in her lap.

The cattle drive wrapped up last week, smooth and successful. Now, every saddle pack is equipped with GPS and an emergency button. Maddie's dad doesn't mess around anymore. When he saw what almost happened to her, he shifted into something just short of military mode. I don't blame him. I respect him for it.

Clara has blossomed. She's taking riding lessons now and already shows she's a natural. She connects with horses the way she connects with people, with soft hands and steady confidence. Watching her trot across the pasture in that helmet and those scuffed boots feels like a miracle. She signs to the horses like they'll answer her, and somehow, they always seem to listen.

This morning, she caught me off guard. She signed that she wants to learn to play drums.

I haven't touched a kit in almost three years.

I told her we'd see. The truth? I miss it. Not the tour buses, the stage lights, or the chaos. But the rhythm. The feel of the sticks in my hands. The peace that came when the beat took over. I've been afraid to go back. Terrified it would lead me into the dark again. But with Clara, it could be something else. Something healing.

She signs again, more certain this time. ***"I want to learn drums. Will you teach me?"***

It knocks the air right out of my chest.

I stare at her and sign, ***"You sure? It's hard."***

She grins. ***"I'm tough like Mom."***

That's it. She's not just asking to learn. She's reaching for me. Trying to build something between us that's hers and mine.

"Then we'll learn together."

Later that night, while Maddie soaks in the tub, muttering something about lavender-scented torture, I sit with Clara at the kitchen table. I pull a folded piece of paper from my pocket. It's the design for a ring. I've been working on it with a local jeweler for months. A raw diamond, set in rose gold. Nothing fancy. Just strong and straightforward. Like her. Like us. I spent too many years stuck in the past. Holding tight to pain and guilt, rereading the same chapters like I could rewrite them if I looked hard enough. But that's not how stories work. You don't start over. You turn the page. You move forward. And I'm ready. I just have one problem: Clara is absolute trash at keeping secrets.

I sign to Clara, ***"Do you want to help me plan something special?"***

She lights up, hands flying. ***"YES. Can we hide it in a goat's mouth? Like a treasure hunt? Or put it in a pancake?"***

I laugh so hard I nearly drop the ring sketch. ***"No pancakes. No goats. You'll eat the ring or traumatize a herd."***

She sticks out her tongue but leans closer, clearly into the mission. ***"What are we doing then?"***

I tell her my idea. The pasture at dusk. Just the three of us. Fireflies. Horses grazing nearby. Something quiet. Intimate.

Clara nods like I've handed her a top-secret mission. ***"Perfect. I'll distract Mom. But I'm not good at secrets."***

"Yeah, I know."

By morning, Maddie's giving us both the side-eye. She taps her foot and says, ***"If either of you is building a goat-sized drum kit in my kitchen, I'm moving out."***

Clara almost signs the whole plan before I throw up my hands like she's betrayed national security.

Maddie laughs, then narrows her eyes. *"You two are terrible liars."*

"We're adorable liars."

She points between us. *"So, are you going to tell me what's going on? Or do I need to bribe it out of you with cookies?"*

Clara looks like she's going to explode. I shake my head and sign, *"You'll see soon. Promise."*

Jude shows up later that day with an envelope, grinning like he just won a bet. He signs, *"You're officially a wealthy man."*

I blink. *"What?"*

"Wild Child Reckless never stopped paying you royalties. I invested most of it while you were in rehab. You're worth more than a few million now."

I just stare at him.

"You mean I've been fixing fence posts and hauling goat feed with millions in the bank?"

He shrugs. *"Seemed like you liked the calmness."*

I shake my head and laugh. I don't want the old life back. But I wouldn't mind a studio.

Maddie walks in just then, eyebrow arched. *"Should I be worried?"*

"Only if you hate music rooms."

She smirks. ***"You mean I get to hear you and Clara banging on drums all day?"***

"You love it."

She rolls her eyes, but her smile says it all. That spark is still there, steadier now, stronger.

Later that night, Clara is asleep, and the house is quiet. Maddie and I sit on the porch swing, her head resting against my shoulder.

"You really okay?" she asks.

"For the first time in years, yeah. I'm not stuck anymore. I used to think the past was all I'd ever have. But books don't read backward. I want to start a new chapter with you."

She looks up at me, soft and still.

I lean in and kiss her forehead. ***"Soon. You'll see."***

And this time, I don't feel like I'm waiting to fall apart. I'm finally coming together.

The sky is streaked with gold and amber, the sun dipping low behind the hills as the last of the daylight kisses the pasture.

Fireflies blink to life in the tall grass. Clara runs ahead in her little boots, her hands signing to the goats like she's their queen.

I trail behind with Maddie, our steps slow. She's still moving stiffly but stronger than ever. Her hand is tucked in mine, warm and certain.

Earlier, I signed that we should take a walk, just the three of us. She didn't question it. Not when Clara lit up like I'd handed her the moon. Not when I led them down the trail past the barn to the south pasture, where we sometimes sit and stargaze.

Clara skips ahead to the little clearing and spins in a circle, laughing before she signs, ***"Now? Now, now?"***

I shake my head, smiling. ***"Not yet. Let her sit. Let it be perfect."***

The quilt is already laid out, soft and worn, the edges stitched by Maddie's grandmother. Mason jars with battery tea lights flicker gently around us. A few goats graze in the distance, blissfully uninterested in the whole thing.

I help Maddie lower to the quilt, her breath hitching just slightly as she eases down. I sit beside her, Clara plopping dramatically between us like she's orchestrating a grand affair. She signs something to Maddie that makes her laugh.

Then Clara signs the signal we rehearsed.

"It's now."

I reach into my jacket pocket and pull out the small velvet box. My hands tremble not with fear, but with everything this moment means. With everything I almost lost. With everything I've found.

Clara moves to stand behind Maddie, throwing her arms wide like a drumroll. Then she turns, pulling something from the tiny goat backpack she insisted on bringing. A sign, hand-painted in Clara's careful lettering, reads: **Will You Marry My Dad?**

Maddie gasps. Her hands fly to her mouth, eyes wide as I kneel awkwardly in the grass, setting the ring box on a blanket in front of her.

"You once told me you'd never trust a drummer."

I pause, watching her eyes fill with tears.

"But I trust you with everything. You and Clara are the only rhythm I need now. I don't want to go back to my past life. I want this one. With you. If you'll have me."

She stares at me, trembling. Then she signs through the tears, *"Yes. Yes. A million times, yes."*

Clara claps wildly, bouncing in place. Then she throws herself into a hug that topples the three of us into a laughing, tangled heap of goat fur, tears, and pure joy.

I slip the ring onto Maddie's finger, the raw diamond catching the last glint of the sun. She stares at it like it's the only thing she's ever wanted.

We don't need music. We don't need an audience.

This is our crescendo.

Chapter 50
Maddie

Later, after the goats are tucked in and Clara's snuggled up in bed, Grayson helps me into mine.

I wince as I lower myself down, biting back the groan. The pain is manageable tonight, but still there is a constant whisper that my body isn't fully mine yet. Not the way it used to be. I hate needing help, but I hate pretending I don't even more. With Grayson, I don't have to.

He doesn't hover. He never does. But he stays close. He pulls the blankets up with careful hands, tucking the edges under my legs the way he knows I like. Then he slips into bed beside me, warm and solid, the scent of him grounding me in a way nothing else can.

I roll onto my side and raise a brow. ***"Are you going to keep looking at me like that?"***

His grin is slow and soft. He signs, ***"Maybe forever."***

I chuckle and press my face into the curve of his neck. His arms wrap around me without hesitation, familiar, protective, sure.

We've shared beds before. Years ago. But this... this is different. There's no rush, no frantic need to close the distance between us. Just warmth. Just peace. Just him, here, exactly where I need him.

His hand moves gently against my back, and he signs without looking up. ***"You're not cleared yet."***

I touch his hand and sign back, ***"I know. But stay anyway."***

"Always."

The lamp clicks off with a soft snap. The room dips into shadow, and I fall asleep to the rhythm of his heartbeat steady against my back.

The scent of bacon and coffee wakes me before the light does.

I shuffle into the kitchen with my cane, still stiff from sleep but steadier than I used to be. Some days, my body fights me harder than others, but this morning is kind. The ache is there, ever-present, but manageable.

Grayson's there in sweatpants, barefoot, and somehow infuriatingly hot as he flips bacon in a skillet. Clara stands beside him at the table, setting out mismatched plates with the kind of flair only a seven-year-old can manage. She's mid-story, her hands a blur of signing as she reenacts what appears to be a theatrical goat escape.

Grayson signs back with practiced ease, one hand occupied with the spatula, the other offering her reactions as he flips bacon like it's a sport.

"Good morning," I sign, leaning on the counter with a yawn.

Clara whips around and points at Grayson, her little hands flying. ***"He's a bacon thief. He ate two already!"***

I arch a brow and level my gaze at him. ***"Stealing from your child now?"***

He shrugs without shame and signs, ***"She's small. She doesn't need a whole serving."***

Clara gasps like he's committed an unforgivable crime. ***"Rude!"***

I laugh so hard that I almost spill my coffee. Everything about this moment feels absurdly normal. The eggs are overdone. The pancakes are lopsided. Clara uses too much syrup. And yet, it feels perfect.

There was a time not long ago when I thought I'd never see mornings like this again, when I wasn't sure I'd even survive the night, let alone wake up to this kind of joy. But here I am. And I don't take a second of it for granted.

Mom arrives home from town just before lunch, and the moment she sees the ring, she gets misty-eyed and cups my face in her hands, kissing my forehead like she used to when I was small with scraped knees. "Oh, baby girl... look at you."

Grayson stands off to the side, awkward but patient, while she peppers me with questions. She hugs him next, firm and long, and tells him in no uncertain terms that he's "stuck with us now."

He shrugs. ***"I could do worse."***

I elbow him, and he grins like the smug idiot he is.

Mom settles in at the table with Clara, who gleefully fills her in on every single detail of the proposal, including the goats. Grayson catches my eye from across the room and signs, ***"I think your mom loves me more than you."***

"Unlikely," I respond, trying not to smile. ***"But possible."***

Dad shows up late in the afternoon, trailing dust, sunburn, and tension in equal measure.

He lingers outside for a beat too long before stepping inside, his gaze sweeping over the room like he's bracing for a fight. When he finally makes his way over to me, he clears his throat and mutters, "Ring's decent. Diamond's clean. Could've gone bigger."

Before I can answer, he looks at Grayson and adds, "At least you're handy with fence repairs."

Grayson nods solemnly. "High praise," I deadpan.

But when I pull my dad in for a hug, he doesn't pull away. Doesn't grunt or backpedal. Just squeeze tight and wordless.

For my father, that says more than anything.

That night, after the day fades and Clara crashes into bed in a sugar coma from the cookies Mom baked that afternoon, I find Grayson on the porch swing. He's barefoot, quiet, watching the stars like he's waiting for them to speak.

I slide in beside him and lean my head on his shoulder. His fingers find mine without hesitation, twining easily.

The stars are especially bright tonight, scattered across the sky like promises waiting to be kept.

He turns slightly and brushes his thumb over my hand before signing. *"I've been thinking. I want to build a house here. On the ranch. Just for us. Close, but separate. Ours."*

The words settle low in my chest, warm and unexpected.

"But," he adds, his eyes locked on mine. *"If you want to leave, I'll go. I'll buy a house anywhere. Wherever you're happiest. This ranch. This town. Doesn't matter. I just want you. Us."*

I stare at him, breath catching. He means it. There's no push. No pressure. Just an open hand.

I reach up, cup his face, and kiss him softly and slowly. *"Building a home here sounds perfect."*

His smile is the kind that builds slowly, like dawn breaking over the horizon. He presses a kiss to my temple and signs, *"Then we start tomorrow. Floor plans. Paint colors. Goat-proof fencing. The works."*

I laugh into his chest and hold him tighter.

The future doesn't feel fragile anymore. It feels like something solid. Something we can build on. Together.

We're not just rebuilding.

We're home.

Chapter 51
Mia

I shouldn't be here.

And if Law says it one more time, I really am going to shove him face-first into a goat pen. He stands beside me, arms crossed, aviators still on even though the sun's already dipped low behind the hills. His expression is carved from stone, jaw tight like he's calculating escape routes. The only real threat here is accidentally stepping in goat poop.

"You're not supposed to be making appearances," he mutters.

I tilt my head and wave a hand at the scene. "It's not an appearance. It's a wedding. With cupcakes. And goats."

"Too many people. Too many unknowns," he says. "You know that."

His voice isn't sharp; it never is when it counts. But it lands just the same. A quiet warning. A reminder I've heard more than once. My gaze flicks across the field: folding chairs, mason jars, neighbors in boots and dresses that still smell like hay. Nothing glamorous. Nothing flashy.

But he's not wrong.

"Still," I say softly, "I needed to be here."

Law doesn't argue. Just exhales through his nose, jaw working as he scans the crowd again. Always watching. Always protecting. He hasn't taken his eyes off the perimeter once. And honestly? I'd be annoyed if it didn't feel so... steady.

"You said we'd keep a low profile," he adds.

"We are," I say, motioning toward the very Pinterest-worthy chaos of the reception. "What's lower profile than a barefoot wedding in a field surrounded by goats and mason jars?"

He lifts an eyebrow. "You've been on the front page of three magazines in the last six weeks."

"Which makes me an excellent distraction," I whisper, smiling sweetly at a goat who's eyeing the cupcake table like it's the promised land.

He doesn't smile. I sigh and add, "Grayson is one of my best friends. I was invited. You don't skip out on people like him. Not after everything."

And I mean it. Grayson signs something to Clara across the yard, gentle hands, maybe. Or be kind to the goat in a bowtie. It's hard to tell. His signing is smooth and confident, the kind that only comes from years of living in the quiet. Maddie answers with a laugh, then signs something back. It's soft. Intimate. Like a conversation built from the marrow of who they are, not just their hands.

I love that for them.

Maddie looks like a fever dream in a dress that drapes more than it sparkles, barefoot, freckled, wildflower petals tangled in her braid. Grayson, in dark jeans and rolled sleeves, somehow manages to look more grounded than I've ever seen him. They said their vows in the pasture. Just the three of them standing barefoot on a quilt from Maddie's grandmother. Clara held a bouquet of wildflowers and signed along through happy tears. Grayson signed his vows slowly, eyes never leaving Maddie's face, and Maddie spoke hers out loud, voice shaking but sure. I don't usually cry at weddings, but I blinked fast enough to blame it on the dust. Or goat dander.

"I know what you're doing," Law says beside me.

I glance at him. "What am I doing?"

He tilts his head toward the couple. "Pretending you don't want something like that."

I scoff. "I don't want goats in my wedding."

He doesn't laugh. Just watches me the way he always does, like he sees through every version of me I try to wear.

"I'm not built for quiet," I say. "Or for... staying."

"You keep saying that," he says calmly. "But you're still here."

I look away. My eyes find Clara spinning near the barn with another kid her age, flower crown askew, arms flung wide like she's trying to catch the whole damn sky. "I signed to Grayson earlier," I say. "Told him he looked good. All grown-up and married off."

"Did you actually say that?"

"Maybe. I might've added I was proud of him too. Don't tell anyone. It'll ruin my image."

Law's lips twitch. "Your secret's safe with me, *Rani.*"

I shoot him a look. "If you call me that again, I'm feeding you to the ring bearer goat."

He leans in just a fraction, voice low. "You say that, but I think part of you likes that someone still sees who you are under all the armor."

I don't answer. Can't. The music picks up again, an acoustic duo Delilah used to play with on weekends now performing under a string of barn lights. This place smells like grass and sweet tea and second chances.

Auntie Celeste would absolutely lose her mind if she saw me now. Standing barefoot on a ranch. Watching a wedding that didn't involve a cathedral or couture. She'd start praying the rosary before the couple even kissed.

But I don't feel out of place. Not here. Not with them. "I'm not ready," I say quietly.

Law doesn't ask what I mean. Doesn't press. He just bumps my shoulder with his, calm and steady. "You don't have to be."

And I nod. Because maybe someday... maybe there's a version of this that fits me too.

No cameras. No chaos. Just someone who stays.

Epilogue
Maddie

The air smells like wildflowers and sweet tea. Somewhere nearby, a goat bleats like it's part of the band warming up near the barn. I'm barefoot in the grass, my hands trembling just enough to make fastening the bracelet a challenge. But it's not nerves. Not really. It's something quieter. Deeper.

Contentment, maybe. Or peace, settling into the cracks I never thought would heal.

"I still think we should've eloped," I murmur, only half-kidding.

Delilah grins at me in the mirror, clipping a tiny spray of baby's breath into my hair. "And miss this aesthetic dream? Not a chance."

My dress drapes softly and simply over my frame, a creamy off-white, Clara picked with near-offensive confidence from a boutique clearance rack. There's no corset, no sparkle, no train. Just the kind of dress that feels like something that moves when I do and doesn't pretend I'm someone I'm not.

"Besides," Delilah says, stepping back, "you've got to win. No rented barn, no matching pastel suits, no one forcing you to use fake doves."

I laugh, remembering the planning war I almost waged with my mother when she floated the idea of a dove release *and* a choreographed dance. Grayson had taken my hand under the table, squeezed once, and then signed, ***"Whatever we do, I want it to feel like us. Simple. Honest. Home."***

So we compromised.

The vows would be outside, in the south pasture, under a string of lights and the watchful eye of a goat named Pickles. The reception would have real food, not tiny, overpriced appetizers. Clara would wear what she wanted, a dress with pockets and flower boots. And the quilt my grandmother stitched years ago? That would be our aisle.

It's not a Pinterest-perfect event. But it's us.

The sun is low when I make my way into the pasture, Clara leading the way with a crown of slightly crooked flowers and a sign that says, "My mom is getting married! Try not to cry!" in big, loopy handwriting.

I spot Grayson before I'm even halfway down the aisle. He's waiting in rolled-up sleeves and dark jeans, the same way he looked when he proposed, steady, sure, already home.

His smile is a little crooked, his hands twitching nervously at his sides before he catches my eye and signs, ***"You look like everything I never knew I needed."***

I blink fast. Crying before I even reach him feels entirely on-brand and altogether inconvenient.

When we stand face to face, the wind gently tugging at my hair and Clara bouncing quietly between us, I can barely hear the officiant. My focus is on Grayson. On his hands as he signs each vow slowly, deliberately, never breaking eye contact. On the feel of the ring, he slides onto my finger, raw diamond, rose gold, no frills. Now, with the matching band.

I speak my vows, voice catching once but steady. I tell him he's the rhythm I'd forgotten how to move to. The stillness I didn't believe I deserved.

Clara slides her hands into ours, linking the three of us like it's the most natural thing in the world. And when we're pronounced married, she throws flower petals like confetti and then signs, ***"Can we eat cake now or what?"***

The reception is as beautifully chaotic as I expected, and nothing like the formal affairs my mother used to dream of. No string quartets. No seating charts. Just fairy lights between fence posts, long tables draped in mismatched linens, and barbecue that leaves half the guests licking their fingers.

Grayson dances with Clara first. She signs something cheeky about his two left feet, and he just laughs, spins her in a slow, clumsy circle, and signs back, ***"I'm better with drums."***

Then he dances with me. Slow. Easy. My head resting against his chest, the beat of his heart the only rhythm I need. The music blurs. The world fades. All I feel is him.

Bow-tied goats wander between guests, one nearly making off with a centerpiece. Later, I catch a glimpse of Mia near the back fence, barefoot in the grass beside a scowling Law. She waves when she sees me watching. I wave back, heart-tugging just a little. She's running from something she won't name yet. I know that look. But I also know she stayed. Which means she hasn't given up. Not entirely. Not like before.

I hope she finds whatever she's chasing.

Grayson kisses me behind the barn while Clara steals frosting from the corner of our tiny homemade cake. We dance barefoot in the grass or sway, really his arms around me, our heads bowed close.

He signs against my shoulder. ***"This is what I meant. When I said I'd stay."***

I pull back to look at him, and my heart does that familiar flip, the one that still surprises me. ***"You didn't just stay,"*** I respond. ***"You built something."***

Later, after the sun dips behind the hills and the fairy lights glow like constellations, Grayson and I sit on the porch swing. Clara's asleep inside, curled up with a stuffed goat someone gave her as a wedding gift.

He reaches for my hand, thumb brushing gently over my fingers as the music drifts low from the barn behind us a sign of the party still going on. Then he signs, ***"Have you ever thought about giving Clara a sibling?"***

My breath catches not from shock, exactly, but from the tenderness of it. The way he asks is without pressure. Without expectation. Just offering it like a shared dream we haven't dared to name yet.

I look over at the window where Clara sleeps inside, curled up with her stuffed goat and remnants of frosting on her cheek. She's already brought so much joy into our lives. Could we really...?

I lean my head on his shoulder and sign, ***"Sometimes I think about it."***

He signs slowly, ***"We'd be a good team. And I think we've got more love to give."***

Tears prick at the corners of my eyes, happy ones, the kind that show up when life surprises you in the best way.

"We'll see," I answer, smiling through it. ***"Maybe after we build that house."***

He laughs, soft and low, pressing a kiss to my temple.

"Deal."

His smile is slow, blooming like it always does when something lands deep for him. Like the first time he saw Clara ride a horse and called her a natural. The past is part of us, always. The pain. The healing. The long road back to each other.

But tonight, we're not defined by any of that. We're something new. Something real.

And we're finally completely home.

From the Author

Thank you for reading!!! If you have a moment please leave a review- they are so incredibly important to indie authors. I always loved reading, and now I have a separate love of writing. I hope you stick around and join me in this amazing adventure! I am always looking to connect! You can find me in the following places.

SmutTok Made Me Do It Facebook Group

Juliet McKinleys Book Nook

Sign Up for my newsletter here so that you never miss a beat, giveaway or sneak peek-

Newsletter   julietmckinley.myflodesk.com

TikTok   @JulieyMcKinleyAuthor

Instagram   @JulietMckinleyAuthor

Facebook   Juliet McKinley

Also by

The Wild Child Reckless Series

This is Growing Up

She was his best friend's little sister and completely off-limits—until one unforgettable night changed everything. Now Delilah is famous, engaged, and untouchable... but Alexander isn't giving up that easily. Because he had her once, and he's not letting her go again.

This is Meant to Be

She's promised to another. He's risking everything to keep her. Lillian was never supposed to fall for Jensen—but now that she has, neither of them is willing to let go, no matter how high the price.

This is Taking Chances *

He shattered her heart once. Now he's back—not just to make amends, but to prove he's worthy of the family he never knew he had. A deaf drummer with a broken past. A single mother who swore she'd never look back. One love story that refuses to stay buried.

This is Starting Over**

She was the one girl he swore off limits. Now she's all grown up, in danger—and back under his protection.

This time, he's not sure he can walk away.

Foster, Inc. Novellas
Jack Frost, CEO

She's his assistant. He's her father's enemy. Pretending to be engaged might save his business deal, but when sparks turn into something real, Jack has to decide if falling for Maisie is worth the risk—or the scandal.

Willow Glen Series
From Feud to Forever*

She stole the land he spent twenty years trying to reclaim. He's determined to make her regret it—until their bickering turns into banter and the sparks start flying. In a small town full of gossip and grudge matches, Adam and Christiane are about to find out that the line between hate and love is thinner than a fence post.

Sons of Santoro Series
Tasting Sin-
Also part of the Sexy as Sin: Las Vegas World

She's the boss with everything to lose. He's the chef with nothing left to prove.

When a high-stakes sabotage threatens Sienna Moreau's Las Vegas hotel, she turns to the one man who infuriates and tempts her in equal measure—Luca Santoro. In a city built on secrets, desire becomes their sharpest weapon... but trusting each other might be the biggest gamble of all.

Monroe Strategic Capital Series

The Christmas Waffle*

He's a grumpy CEO with a plan for everything. She's the too-young, off-limits assistant who blows it all to hell with one unforgettable night—and one life-changing surprise. Now, with secrets, misunderstandings, and a baby on the line, they'll have to decide if their second chance is worth risking everything for.

*2025 $0.99 Preorder

** 2026 $0.99 Preorder